CASH LARAMIE and the SUNDOWN EXPRESS

featuring CALVIN CARTER

Edward A.
GRAINGER * Scott Dennis
PARKER

The authors wish to thank Nik Morton
for his guiding insight.

Contents

1899
WYOMING

Special Delivery

Ashdale, Wyoming: Mid-morning

The sound arrived first. The distinctive rumble of an iron horse roaring over steel rails, carried on the wind to the ears of the people gathered at the Ashdale Station. Sheriff Roy Tanner frowned. Something was wrong. He knew it, and, based on the faces of the others lingering on the platform, they knew it, too.

A train was coming, but it was coming from the wrong direction.

Like many of the citizens of the town, Sheriff Tanner had turned out to watch the inaugural run of the trailblazing-in-design train dubbed the *Sundown Express*, capable of a speed topping seventy miles an hour. The crowd had stuck around, braving the sweltering August heat, to prattle on over the sight of the mighty locomotive as it sped through their small community, destined for Sioux Falls. Tanner had even taken pity on Edwin Curtis, a swarthy prisoner whose penchant for robbing trains earned him a trial date as soon as the judge returned to Ashdale. Handcuffed together, wrist to wrist, Tanner could tell Curtis also sensed something.

"I thought the paper said the track was gonna be cleared for the *Express*," Curtis said.

"That's right," the sheriff replied. The lawman reached into a trouser pocket, removed a bandana, and began wiping the sweat from his forehead and neck.

The sound grew louder. From a distance, through the shimmering heat waves rising from the flat land, a dark shape moved.

A handful of people stepped forward to the edge of the platform, curious. Without warning, Curtis stepped forward, too, craning his neck over the heads of the onlookers and yanking on Tanner's arm, but the lawman didn't much care. He wanted to see as well. He recognized the distinctive outline of a train approaching. The plume of smoke rose from the stack and caromed into the wind.

Tanner glanced over his shoulder at the ticket clerk. The scrawny, short man frowned and squinted his eyes behind a pair of spectacles, absently scratching his head as he checked the schedule from his seat inside the tiny ticket booth.

"Neville," Tanner called to the clerk, "what train is this?"

"I don't know. There can't be another train due from the east until the *Express* crosses into Dakota Territory. That'll be hours from now."

Curtis hmphed. "Schedule or not, that train's almost here. And it ain't slowing down." He gestured with his chin. "It's the *Express* again."

Tanner gawked at the outlaw. "How do you know?"

"The speed. I ain't never heard anything move that fast."

"There ain't a turnaround for at least a hundred miles," the sheriff scoffed. "Only way for it to be the *Express* was if it was going backwards."

Neville let out a panicked laugh, masking a deepening alarm. "But why would it be coming back here, going in reverse no less?"

Moments later, the caboose rocketed in, its gold-and-red paint confirming Curtis's assertion, followed quickly by the passenger cars with "Sundown Express" emblazoned on the sides. Unlike its first pass, the train didn't slow down this time, and, from the open doors of a boxcar, a bundle was tossed through the air. Tanner didn't need but a glance to recognize the shape as a bound and gagged man.

Startled bystanders bounded across the platform boards in chaos, rushing out of harm's way. When the body hit the planks, it rolled several times before smashing into the wooden ticket booth and dislodging the shocked clerk from his seat.

As the train steamed onward to Cheyenne, a stunned silence briefly fell in its wake, only to be broken when a few folks began murmuring about what they had just witnessed. Tanner, hardened by the Great Unpleasantness, stood speechless until the moaning of the victim roused him from his stupor.

The discarded man, lying on his back, raised his bloodied head a fraction then lowered it, fixed gray eyes staring upon oblivion.

Needing no prompt, the paling clerk righted himself and backed away from the corpse in an ungainly scramble.

Sheriff Tanner unlocked the handcuff from his wrist and reattached it to a porter's cart handle. "Stay put," he told his prisoner.

"I ain't goin' nowhere," Curtis said. He stood rooted in place and gazed west at the rapidly disappearing *Sundown Express*, something akin to respect showing on his face.

Tanner ran to the wrecked ticket stand and lowered himself to one knee beside the portly man dressed in a brown and tan chalk-stripe suit. There was a wide patch of blood on the victim's vest, a gut shot, which didn't bode well. Neither did the taut leather cord tied around his throat. Tanner pressed two fingers to the side of the man's neck.

"Is he, is he dead?" Neville asked as he steadied himself on what remained of the ticket booth.

The lawman nodded solemnly. He pulled at the leather cord, revealing an envelope tucked inside the man's vest. It read simply: "For Senator Madison."

"Is that a message?" Neville said.

"No," Curtis said, his lips curling over his teeth into a wide grin. "It's a ransom."

CHAPTER 1

Hare-Brained Mission

Cheyenne, Wyoming: An hour later

Senator Daniel Madison's hands worried across the brim of his hat as he sat in the office of Devon Penn, chief of the marshal service in Cheyenne. Penn's office was well appointed with dark paneled wood lining the walls, several floor-to-ceiling, built-in bookcases, and a colorful Mexican rug adorning the floor. A massive, taxidermied bison head had been mounted over the door, and the chief's saber from the war hung above the fireplace mantle. Dozens of dinosaur bone fossils were displayed in glass curio cabinets that filled the spaces between bookcases. The entirety spoke to the chief's passion for collecting.

Penn was seated in an armchair behind his mahogany desk, a black homburg hat placed on top of some papers. His black frock coat was open revealing a white shirt, a black tie, and green suspenders.

In the chair next to the senator, a man in a crisp, medal-decorated uniform sat straight and tall.

"Welcome, gentlemen," Penn addressed in a booming voice. "Senator Madison, this is Army Colonel Isaac Furlow. Behind you are two of my best deputy marshals, Cash Laramie and Gideon Miles." The senator and colonel both glanced over their shoulders, and exchanged brisk greetings with Cash, who stood leaning against the office doorframe, and Miles, who rested on the windowsill that overlooked the main street.

Penn continued, "As you know, time is of the essence. Immediately upon receiving the telegram with the grave news, I called all of you here to discuss a course of action."

He swiveled in his chair and pointed to a map on the wall behind him, tracing a line in the air. "The *Express*'s selling point is that at full speed, it can cover the 520 miles between Cheyenne and Sioux Falls in about eight hours, allowing for one stop at a fueling station. It economizes on the need for sleeper cars, and instead that space can be allocated to carrying additional paying customers."

"Who cares about that!" The senator held out a blood-stained letter, his hands trembling, beads of perspiration forming at the edges of his neatly cut, tawny hair. "This is the immediate quandary—this letter sent by courier. It had been fastened to the late Mr. Roger Halsworth, addressed to me, conveying an ultimatum."

"Very true. We have a reasonable idea of what we're up against," the chief said. "The *Sundown Express* was seized by a gang of murdering marauders who have demanded $100,000, in cash, by seven o'clock this evening."

"Is that their little joke—that's sunset, isn't it?" Miles suggested.

"Whether or not it is, it isn't funny. If we don't comply, they will kill even more passengers. Mr. Halsworth was the unfortunate first. He'd been shot in the gut before being callously tossed from the train."

Cash murmured, "Who was it that said, 'Don't shoot the messenger?'"

Penn flashed an unappreciative look at Cash, glossing over the imprudent comment. "The *Express* is packed with politicians, newspapermen, railroad administrators, and, God help us, actress Lillie Langtry."

"Not to forget my daughter, Jessica," Senator Madison cut in, his dove-gray eyes steadfast on Penn.

"Yes, Senator Madison's presence here should remind everyone of the dire seriousness of the issue." Penn nodded, belying the exasperation showing on his round face, though the distraught politician hardly seemed to catch on.

In all the times that Cash had been doled out missions in the chief's office, he had rarely known it to harbor such palpable tension. Undoubtedly, the senator's status contributed to the uneasy atmosphere.

"How did the culprits get aboard?" Miles asked. "Surely passengers would have been hand selected or vetted."

The senator shook his head. "We don't know. Tickets were sold by invitation only. This was a highly prestigious event for Cheyenne, and, given these circumstances, we rightfully hired a railroad detective." He shifted in his seat and slapped a hand on the upholstered arm. "Do we really need to go over all this?" he barked. "What we need now is a rescue plan, Chief Penn."

"Easier said than done, Senator—" a knock on the office door interrupted him.

"Enter," Penn called.

Cash opened the door to a smartly dressed civilian in a brown tweed suit standing there. The man removed his derby hat and spoke rapidly. "You sent for me, Chief Penn. I'm Joseph Latimer, Cheyenne train inspector."

"Ah, yes." Penn waved Latimer forward. "Come in and please tell us briefly about the rolling stock of the *Sundown Express*."

Latimer walked up to the side of Penn's desk. He cleared his throat then fired off in one breath: "Well, sir, the *Express* has ten cars in total. There's the locomotive engine itself, its fuel tender, then you have the dining car with the galley, then the luxury salon car as it's called, then you have two private cars—each with four compartments apiece—and the boxcar, then two passenger cars with central aisles, and finally the caboose." He gulped, drawing in some air. "That's the full stock, sirs."

"Kind of a short train," Cash observed.

Latimer said, "The remaining cars are being readied for full passenger service later this month, sir."

"Thank you, Mr. Latimer," Penn said. "That is exactly what we need to know."

Latimer nodded to Penn and everyone in turn as he pivoted on his heel and left.

Miles folded his arms. "It wouldn't take many outlaws to cover and control so few cars."

"True," Cash said. "How do these varmints expect to get the ransom?"

"They've stipulated that it must be put in several carpet bags and left at the fueling station. There's a small township close by." Penn pointed to a dot on the map.

Colonel Furlow chimed in, "That would be a good place where we can lie in wait for them."

Penn shook his head. "It's not going to be that simple. They've warned us that not only do they have a passel of accomplices at the stopover, apparently they've also waylaid a stagecoach with additional captives."

The senator squeezed the bloodstained letter. "They've thought of everything, it seems." He appeared to choke down something hard, as if he'd swallowed a chicken bone.

Penn reflexively cleared his throat. "We've come to the tricky part. While the marauders wait for the payoff, we know they are planning to run the train forward and back along a section of track across these fifty miles of open country." He used both hands to span the section on the map.

Cash straightened his six-foot-one frame. "Keeping on the move over that exposed stretch, the bandits have a clear view for miles. If they see us attempting a rescue, it could trigger more killings."

Senator Madison's face reddened. "I wish you wouldn't talk of *killings*."

"Sorry, Senator," Cash replied. Just like politicians, he pondered, to only be concerned when their own interests were at risk.

"This fifty-mile section where they keep going back and forth, why did they choose that particular length of track?" Miles asked.

"It passes just two stations. The nearest end is where they delivered their grisly message with Mr. Halsworth's body," Penn said. "Presumably, if they decide to, they will deliver other sickening messages there, too. At the far end is the fueling station I mentioned, just before a junction in the track. I can only surmise they've blocked access on those other lines."

"Okay," Cash said. "Going back to the open country. I reckon there's one exception, isn't there?" He stepped around the desk and tapped an area of the map darkened by a cluster of swirls. "There's a narrow mountain range here. Looks to be about a two-mile stretch where the tracks tunnel into it. On the other side, the train goes down a gradual descent into open country, and five miles further is the besieged fueling station."

"Exactly, you've hit upon it," Penn said. "That's why Colonel Furlow is here. You see, there's a slim chance we can get you and Miles on the *Express*."

Miles crossed his arms against his boxer's frame and shot a knowing look to his partner then back to Penn. "Slim? *How slim?*"

Penn turned to the colonel. "Would you be willing to explain it to my deputies?"

The hawkish, blond-haired Furlow leaned forward in his chair. "There is an artificial break in the mountain, approximately a quarter of a mile in. As the engineers were excavating the tunnel, an unexpected soft spot in the ground opened up from above, accidentally leaving behind a twelve-foot-wide shaft that goes straight up to the outside." He stopped and looked at Penn.

Penn said, "We could lower some people through the opening onto the moving train."

"Lower people?" Miles said, his tone growing contentious. "Onto a speeding train without being seen?"

"It's in the tunnel. We won't be seen," Cash said, with an air of nonchalance as if he was describing the weather.

"Yeah, right, I was forgetting." Miles rolled his eyes.

Cash gave a low whistle. "Still, it's cutting it fine."

Miles nodded. "It sure is. The train will take just under two minutes to pass through the tunnel. Even if it slows down, like most trains do in a tunnel, we're expected to get on its moving roof in that time?"

"Yes," Penn said.

Miles glowered. "How do you propose we do that?"

Cash interjected. "There's no way we would have the time to get up that monster of a mountain. We'd need pack mules and equipment."

Penn beamed with pride at his men, the best he'd ever commanded as they weighed options. "You're right. We'd need a lot of time and a lot of equipment, and plan for just the right minute to even attempt a feat such as this. The mountain itself is quite steep, so we would need climbing gear to scale the side to say nothing of then using that same equipment to lower you through the shaft and into the tunnel. It is nearly impossible. But what if I told you there's another way?" He paused and arched an eyebrow. "Colonel?"

Furlow pulled a pipe from his left pocket, packed it with tobacco, and was about to ignite a match.

"Colonel?" Penn said, heightening his voice.

Furlow lowered his pipe to the desk. He pursed his lips as if reluctant to speak further.

"President McKinley wants our service to handle this," Penn persisted, eyeing the officer. "They'll have to know."

Furlow relented. "Very well. Gentlemen, the military has been working with a scientist on an advanced airship dubbed *The Pegasus*. It is outfitted with the latest weapons, but the real pride of *The Pegasus* is a system of pulleys attached to mirrors that can render it nearly invisible among the clouds." He chuckled. "I could sit here and blab all day and still not begin to explain it to you. Its inventor, Professor Blaylock, is a genius."

Miles glanced at Cash. "Maybe that explains the mystery shapes in the sky that everyone was reporting a while back. Even talk of beings paying us a visit from another planet."

"This is poppycock!" exclaimed the senator.

"Actually, I liken it to something straight out of Jules Verne," observed the colonel.

"I tend to agree," Penn said. "It's no different than when the first submarine was being developed. Folks swore they saw otherworldly beasts roaming the seas and predicted the end of times were at hand. Problem is if you start telling the public the truth about these inventions, the enemy will eventually catch wind of it and move heaven and earth to steal the designs to use against us."

"Spoken like a true military man, Chief Penn," Furlow said. "*The Pegasus*, or a fleet of these airships, could rule the sky, and America would attain superior domination for a century or more." His reached for his pipe but retracted as Penn's stare lanced into him. He turned sideways to look at the senator, adding, "I'm sorry to say, but I'm against the president using *The Pegasus* for such a hare-brained mission as Chief Penn proposes."

Senator Madison shot him an aggravated glance.

"Now, Senator," the colonel said, raising his hands in mollifying fashion, "I mean no disrespect, and I sympathize with your daughter's predicament, but national interests are at stake, and I feel this is a matter best handled by simple negotiation."

"I think not," Madison snapped. "The blatant evidence is before us: a body was already tossed on the railway platform, and you can bet if we don't deliver the ransom money more innocents will be murdered—my daughter could be next. Their first act shows utter contempt for any form of negotiation. Let us not allow there to be a second."

"Gentleman, there is no reason to quarrel," Penn said. "It has been already decided." He gestured at Cash and Miles. "You will follow Colonel Furlow to a secret government site which the army has designated Area 53 near Red Feather Lakes."

"You mean the government has that many secret sites?" Miles asked.

"No, no. As I understand it, the numbering system starts at fifty. To date there are fifty-six dispersed around the country," Penn explained. "Once you're there, you'll meet Professor Blaylock and make preparations to take back the *Express*."

"Yes, sir," the pair replied in unison.

"And with minimal loss of captives, I might add."

"Oh, dear God," moaned the senator, sotto voce.

CHAPTER 2

All Tied-Up

Earlier that morning.

A throng of people had congregated on the Cheyenne platform, all admiring the sparkling new engine and the smart red, yellow, and brown livery of the cars it hauled, and reveling in the festive atmosphere surrounding the train's premiere.

Decked in the finest dresses and tailored suits, the most notable guests on the passenger list gathered in a group next to the glistening engine, posing for photographs to be published in the *Cheyenne Leader*. Among them stood famed actress Lillie Langtry. She easily garnered the most attention while Cheyenne's mayor, sheriff, and a few local politicians each took turns standing awkwardly by the gracious, smiling actress, her radiance outshined only by the intensity of the day's sweltering sun.

After photographs had been taken and speeches given, they were first to board, climbing into the luxury salon at the front of the train. A select few, rumored to be investors and railroad administrators, climbed into the two private compartments right behind the luxury salon and just forward of the boxcar.

While the special guests boarded with their printed invitations issued by the *Cheyenne Leader*, the remaining passengers grew restless. About half of them were local citizens, rich enough to afford a ticket but not wealthy enough to procure a private cabin with velvet-covered plush seats. Still, they carried themselves with an air of self-importance.

Rounding out the passenger cars were people who'd won a lottery that had been organized by the newspaper. The entry requirement was to have purchased a copy of the paper, torn off the entry slip on the last page, filled out a name, and returned it back to the newsroom. A public ceremony in which the editor of the paper, a rugged man named Hector who looked nothing like a newspaper editor, reached into a large glass bowl and withdrew the entry slips. Star newsman Emil Emerson unfolded the slips and read aloud the handpicked entrants, and an earnest young lady, Hector's daughter, wrote down the winners on a list that was later posted on the bulletin board outside of the newspaper's office.

This last group jostled forward, eager to claim their prizes and be among the first riders on the *Sundown Express*. Each and every one of them were smartly dressed in the best they could afford. Nothing as luxurious as the folks in the private cars, but certainly their Sunday best. They filed in, took their seats, chattering the entire time. Excitement spread through the cars like electricity, punctuated by cheers as the steam engine lurched away from the station.

One man didn't make a sound. He merely grinned as his eyes fell on each member of his gang. Sid Banning had thought of everything. He allowed himself to relax as the *Express* was soon beyond the limits of the city and traveling through the colorful open range.

Banning's plan called for the initial excitement of the ride to wash over the passengers. He had told his gang of men the first quarter hour wouldn't be a good time to take the train. Everyone would be too keyed up, looking at all the fixtures and marveling at the speed. Only after the passengers settled down to ride would it be the optimal time.

When that moment came, Banning nodded at Morgan Miller, a big man who had arrived at Cheyenne with a bandolier of shells draped around his chest. Looking more than a mite conspicuous, Banning had ordered him to lose the shells or cover them. "We don't want to tip our hand," Banning had said. Grumbling the entire time, Miller had bought a long duster and a vest out of necessity and ended up appreciating the clothing as they nicely hid both the bandolier shells and the Winchester.

Miller rose from his seat and moved leisurely along the aisle to the rear of the car. Everybody seemed so intent on the passing scenery that nobody noticed him slip through the door that led to the caboose. That put their guardsman in place.

Next, Banning got up from his seat. Orville "Hoop" Hooper, Abe Stone, Karl Wilde, Mule Dunn, and the two Yates brothers joined him, moving forward to the interconnecting door with its glass panel. Banning peered through briefly—all clear—then opened the door, allowing his men to pass through while he gestured to Zeke Perkins who rose from his seat and made his way to the rear. Banning closed the door. The noise of the train between cars was deafening and the wind-blast severe. He clamped a hand hard on his brown derby.

Before crossing into the next car, Banning checked with the men gathered in the small space that they were sure about their tasks, shouting to be heard. "You got this, Hoop?"

"Damn straight," barked Hoop. "While Zeke holds up the passengers back of us, I'll do the same in this car."

Banning smiled. One man with a gun should be enough in the confined aisles. "What about you two?" he asked, looking toward the brothers.

Toby and Teddy Yates nodded in unison, with Teddy adding in his Arkansas drawl, "We'll take the boxcar—and the mail guys."

"I'll deal with the private compartments," Karl chimed in.

"I'll stick with you, boss," said Abe.

"Me, too," said Mule.

"Good. Let's go!" Banning led them from one coupling platform to the next, opening the door onto another passenger car with a central aisle. A few eyes studied them briefly, but the majority of the people were gawking at the flat expanse of land. As agreed, Hoop wouldn't make his move until Banning and the rest were out of sight.

Shutting the door behind them, Banning stepped across the gap and entered the boxcar.

One sidewall of the car comprised a counter with sorting pigeonholes for mail, some of which were already filled. Three large bundles of sealed sacks were clustered on the floorboards while another was gaping open. On the opposite side hung several loops of rope. Tethered to brackets, there were a number of wooden crates, all labeled "whiskey."

Two mailmen were drawn by the sound from outside and looked up as Banning stepped in.

"You shouldn't be here, sir," the tall, balding mailman shouted above the noise of the train.

Banning swept back his jacket and pulled his right-hand revolver. "This says I should." He waggled the gun at them as Toby, Teddy, Abe, Mule, and Karl entered behind him. "Don't reach for any weapon. The mail ain't worth your life."

As one, the pair raised their hands.

"That's sensible." Banning turned to Karl. "You're good with knots. Tie them up."

"Sure, boss," Karl replied, retrieving a couple of lengths of rope and winding the pieces around the mailmen until they were incapacitated.

"All right, Toby, Teddy. Start going through the mailbags, see what you can find," Banning ordered.

"Hey," said Toby, digging into the bag that was already open, "it's like a birthday and Christmas rolled into one!"

"You are *so* simple," snarled Teddy.

Banning said, "Put a cinch on your jaws, guys. Whatever you find is bonus. Now, Abe, Mule, you're with me. Karl, bring plenty of rope."

"This is *too* easy," Karl said, draping coils of rope over his shoulder.

"Getting the ransom money's the hard part," Banning said, crossing the gap to the next car.

He opened the door onto a corridor that ran one side of the car. The other side comprised four adjoining private compartments. Every one of them had their blinds drawn on the corridor side, which made life easier, Banning reckoned. "We tackle one compartment at a time."

Gun in one hand, Abe slid the first open. "Well, fancy meeting you two here," he whispered hoarsely.

Two smartly dressed, armed fellows stood over three unconscious men lying on the floor by the compartment's window. Their names, Greene and White, sounded like a vaudeville act, but they'd been posing as businessmen to obtain access, all part of Banning's impeccable planning.

Abe glanced over his shoulder. "I wondered where they'd got to."

Banning grinned. "I don't put all my eggs in one basket." He signaled to Karl, and then pointed to the unconscious men. "Gag and truss them up."

"Sure, boss."

The second compartment beckoned. Abe slid open this door. Banning took off his derby and gave it to him.

Four middle-aged men and two young women all gazed out the window at a verdant slope of ponderosa and blackjack pine. A redheaded woman craned her neck at Abe's entrance and her face went pale at the sight of the outlaws and their guns. Her mouth opened but no sound came out.

"Be obliging," Banning said, "and empty your pockets and purses."

At those words, the other woman and the men turned.

"Come on," Abe said, "just keep quiet and put your belongings into this hat."

"You won't get away with this!" berated a stout fellow.

"Do as I say, and no one will get hurt." Abe shook the empty derby.

Reluctantly, the stout man removed a wallet and a derringer from his jacket and a fob watch from his vest, dropping them in the hat.

"Excellent," said Banning.

The women emptied their small purses, and the other men contributed the contents of their pockets, by which time the derby was quite heavy.

"Now, folks," Abe said, "please sit down while my friend ties you up."

Karl shoved past him. "You're too damned polite, kid." He looped the rope around the captives' hands behind their backs and then bound their ankles. When he lingered in securing the redheaded woman, sliding a hand up her stockinged calf, she kicked him hard in the shin with the pointed toe of her laced boot. Karl swore, rubbing his leg.

Banning scowled at him, then stepped in and helped to hold the woman's legs while Karl finished tying her ankles. "Don't take all day, man. We've got another seven compartments to secure," He looked at his hat nearly brimming over with loot. "We should've brought a bag from the boxcar."

Karl stood up. "We're gonna need more rope, too."

"Use their shoelaces, belts, ribbons, anything," said Banning, the irritation evident in his voice. He realized he hadn't planned for everything after all. He consoled himself with the thought that these were minor issues, and he'd planned for the major things, for sure. Right now, he expected Prout and Krebbs were in control of the engine.

* * *

In Cheyenne, Prout and Krebbs had boarded the train's galley that was situated at the front section of the dining car. Dressed in black pants, white shirts, and black vests, they were posing as the caterers, having commandeered the food wagon of the two actual caterers and disposed of their bodies in a back alley.

Once the train was underway, they held up at gunpoint the two chefs and the waiter, who had all been lounging against the counter enjoying a bite from the griddle. The heating came from gas cylinders, Prout noted, his stomach rumbling at the delicious smell of bacon. Lately, he'd always been hungry. He had the gut to prove it. The black vest barely contained his rotund frame. If things got rough, a button or two would likely pop off.

While Prout covered them with his six-gun—and happily snacked on the bacon—Krebbs used strips of apron to tie and gag the three men. With only the dining room separating them from the next rear car, the so-called luxury salon, Banning had been specific about no gunfire or shouting from the captives. No noise. "We want to surprise our honored sojourners."

Prout licked his lips. His mouth was dry. It was the hot weather—or maybe the tension of the holdup was getting to him. He thought how he'd dearly love a shot of bourbon. As if echoing his longing, he heard glasses clinking. He hunkered down at the counter that butted the wall to the dining area. There was a servery hatch, virtually fully closed, with only a gap at the bottom. He squinted through. His heart started to hammer.

Dressed in a tidy, black-and-white tuxedo, with a cluster diamond-pin and yellow tie, a man with a moustache and slicked-back hair was polishing wine glasses and placing them on the tables.

Unable to speak, Prout signaled to Krebbs.

"What is it?" Krebbs whispered.

"We forgot about the barkeep," he croaked. "If he comes in here and sees all them trussed up, we're in a heap of trouble."

"All right. You stay and deal with the barkeep if he comes in. I'll go and take the engine crew."

"You sure?"

Krebbs grinned. "They're probably not even armed."

"The fireman'll have a big shovel."

Whipping out his Colt, the shorter man said, "I have a bigger gun."

"You sure they'll go backward when we hit the agreed spot?"

"There's two of them. If one gets shot, the other will be only too happy to obey."

"Yeah." Yet an unfathomable nagging doubt troubled Prout, churning his stomach.

Krebbs made his way to the other end of the galley and opened the door onto the iron-plate coupling platform. Before the door shut, Prout glimpsed the tender piled high with coal. Krebbs had a hell of a scramble over that filthy stuff. Rather him than me, Prout thought.

Straightening up, he wondered if there was any booze in one of the galley's cupboards.

CHAPTER 3

A Precarious Profession

When railroad detective Calvin Carter received the assignment from his commanding officer, he had taken no small amount of pride that he was requested by name. Well, not necessarily by name. More by reputation. For the inaugural run of the *Sundown Express*, the owner wanted security to be kept at a minimum and mostly out of sight. It wouldn't do to have the fastest train in the west look like it was an army train. The executives of the *Express* wanted someone who could blend in with the bigwigs and not appear like a lawman. Few badge totters could fit that bill, but for Carter, a former actor, it was natural.

Only a few men knew Carter was a detective. Others took him at face value in his guise as an actor, and it was an easy part to play. In fact, it was a role he had played since he was a boy and, with his mother's encouragement, had developed under a series of tutors. He had even played in Cheyenne when he traveled around the country with an acting troupe, so he knew the town well. Carter chose the best hotel to book a room, had little problem convincing the editor of the *Cheyenne Leader* to let the detective monitor the drawing of names, and even had the opportunity to take the editor's daughter out to dinner.

Now, in the forward salon car, he took a moment to appreciate the fine interior. It was richly appointed, with thick carpeting, gray and mauve flock wallpaper, and highly polished and ornate wood walls with shining brass fittings. There were a dozen plush upholstered armchairs scattered about, with small tables, and several stools by the bar at the far end. Two skylights in the ceiling offered additional daylight. Red velvet tasseled drapes adorned the windows, swept aside by matching tiebacks. Electric lights with shades were spaced along the ceiling on the two sides of the car.

This was a far cry from how he traveled during his acting days. Hell, it was even better than how he traveled on most of his assignments. He could certainly get used to this.

He inhaled deeply and looked around the room. As a matter of course, he had identified everyone present.

First was the celebrated actress Lillie Langtry, whose beauty belied her forty-six years. Her deep blue eyes were those of an enchantress, while her long auburn, almost Titian hair fell in appealing curls to her bare shoulders. Her skin and complexion was pale, like a peach. Trimmed with white lace, the fulsome bodice and narrow waist of her tight green silk dress revealed a stunning figure. Carter ran a hand through his dark hair. He could well understand why her admirer, Oscar Wilde, had declared: "I would rather have discovered Mrs. Langtry than have discovered America."

She had taken the part of Rosalind in *As You Like It* at the Cheyenne Theater, her appearance ensuring all five hundred seats were occupied. While the critics were lukewarm, the audience loved her. During her brief time in the city, the reception lobby of the Inter-Ocean Hotel, where she stayed, was inundated with people anxious to get a glimpse of her.

Mr. Frederick Gebhard was never far from her. He was her manager and reputedly her lover, which scandalized certain sections of society, but not those who paid to see her act. Gebhard appeared several years younger than Lillie, slight of frame, with delicate features, a straight nose above a small dark-brown moustache, and a rounded chin. His hair was the same brown, cut short. He wore a black swallowtail coat that could easily have him mistaken for an undertaker. He was very attentive to her, and the cast of his features suggested he resented the men Lillie inevitably attracted.

Of course, in the minds of certain people, they were more important than a mere actress of dubious repute. One such was Mr. Warren Sykes, the owner of the *Sundown Express*. In his sixties, Carter guessed, Sykes was short in stature, with weak brown eyes and smartly cut salt-and-pepper hair. He wore a typical gray-striped business suit and an ostentatious mauve bowtie. Sykes waxed lyrical about his train. Carter caught the odd enthusiastic technical item: "You will be aware many trains have used oil lamps for internal lighting. A couple of years ago the *Florida Special* and the *Chicago Limited* employed electricity supplied by steam-driven generators in the boxcar. We, however, have opted for generating electricity by using a dynamo driven from axles under our cars which charge lead-acid batteries. Voila!" He flicked a switch and the overhead lights flickered on.

Carter switched off.

Doubtless vying for important precedence, but without the attraction of being an "enlightening technician," was Mr.

Roger Halsworth, an executive of the *Sundown Express* in his early fifties. He was bald with a ruddy complexion and piercing gray eyes.

The only other woman in this car was Miss Jessica Madison, the senator's daughter. She was in her early twenties and of medium height. Despite her youth, in contrast to Lillie, she was no great beauty, but her high cheekbones were distinctive and her cornflower blue eyes held promise. She exhibited a coquettish mannerism of twirling a finger through her blonde ringlets. She amply filled her cream silk chemise, white button-down blouse, bouffant skirt, and green velvet bolero jacket. She seemed to fidget, nervously crossing and uncrossing her legs, to reveal black ankle-high boots and the occasional flash of a cream petticoat trim.

Propping up the bar in the time-honored fashion were two stalwart newspaper men, Emil Emerson and Upton Holtman, blatantly glad of the complimentary drinks. Emerson from the *Cheyenne Leader* had a luxuriant red moustache and thick side whiskers, while Holtman from the *Wyoming Eagle* wore wire spectacles and a large polka-dot bowtie. Earlier, they had chatted with Jessica, who explained she was a freelance journalist. "My idol is Nellie Bly," she gushed. "Her in-depth insider articles on the Blackwell Island asylum were sensational."

Emerson snorted, his moustache billowing, and dismissed her with the comment, "You're just stunt girls. Not proper journalists."

"No," said Holtman, "I disagree. It took guts for Bly to get admitted and stay in those deplorable conditions for over a week."

Emerson gulped his whiskey and asked the bartender for another, then added, "She's been nothing but show since her *Around the world in 80 Days* stunt."

"You're welcome to your opinion, sir," Jessica replied calmly. "But I believe she writes very well indeed—*and* sells copy." She paused as Emerson spluttered on his drink and Holtman patted the man's back.

Carter turned his attention to four minor politicians. With only a cursory glance while they boarded the train, Carter had pegged the profession of Allbeury, Pelletier, Rendell and Vincenzi as politicians. Each man wore a fancy black suit, matching black vest, with pocket watch chains hanging from the vest pockets. Their hair was perfectly coiffed so as to withstand a stiff breeze and move not a strand. About the only thing distinctive were the tie colors: Allbeury, Pelletier, and Rendell chose gray while Vincenzi sported a red tie. They occupied upholstered armchairs and smoked cheroots while swapping filibustering stories. Carter believed they were only here to get their photograph in the newssheets, preferably alongside Miss Langtry.

Amid a cloying smoky fug hovering at the ceiling of the salon car, everyone was in high spirits. At the outset, the politicians had fawned over Lillie at the bar. With little prompting she regaled them about a tragic episode: "Almost a year ago, I do recall."

For verification, she gestured at Gebhard sitting alone with his tumbler of gin nearby. He nodded. "Yes, we were traveling in my private car on an Erie Railroad express bound for Chicago. Another railcar carried seventeen of our fine horses." She dabbed an eye with a lace handkerchief, though no tear had appeared. Ever the actress, Carter thought with admiration. "I don't know how it happened, but the horse car was derailed in the early hours of the morning. It rolled down a high embankment and burst into flames!"

"Good lord!" exclaimed Rendell.

"Only one man died—and that too was the sad fate of dear Frederick's champion runner and fourteen other horses of ours."

"How tragic, indeed," said Pelletier, shaking his bald head in commiseration.

She nodded, swallowed. "Ironically, one of the two surviving horses was called St. Savior. He was named after our little church in Jersey, where my father had been rector."

"Almighty strange, ma'am," concurred Allbeury, stroking his lantern jaw. "What town in New Jersey?"

She smiled. "The Channel Islands. The United Kingdom."

All the while, Holtman the journalist scribbled in his notebook, constantly licking the lead end of his pencil. Carter amused himself with the thought that the newsman's moustache looked like some exotic animal gnawing on a stick. Emerson, perhaps having heard too many of the actress's stories, moved off with Halsworth, the pair quietly talking.

Shortly afterward, she had tired of their attention and begged them to give her space.

They grudgingly agreed and she left their company to seat herself in a chair beside Gebhard. She took up her book.

Carter tentatively approached her. "They are dripping with praise for you, Miss Langtry," he said. "Though they remind me of a speech from *She Stoops to Conquer*: 'Those who have most virtue in their mouths, have least of it in their bosoms.'"

"Ah, yes." She chuckled appreciatively. "The Marlow character. Well remembered, sir."

He smiled, quite pleased with himself to have dredged up that quotation. "I wonder if I might have your autograph?" he asked, proffering a fountain pen.

"Yes, of course. I recall overhearing that you are an actor as well. Is that so?"

Carter smiled. "That's right. But not as gifted as you."

She tilted her head slightly. "No need to flatter when it's just us wandering thespians."

Widening his grin, Carter said, "It is only the truth. I've seen your work. You are genuinely one of the greatest actors of our time."

She had the charm to entice a hermit from his cave or tempt an angel from his high estate. His heart beat against his chest as he tilted his head, trying to read her book's title.

She giggled delightfully. "I'm thinking of getting a playwright to interpret this for the stage." She held up the book: *Bella Starr, the Bandit Queen, or the Female Jesse James*.

"Ah, yes, based on the life of the outlaw, though the author's changed the spelling of her name," he said. "There was a mystery about her death, I believe."

"I wouldn't know. I haven't got that far in the novel yet." She lowered the book to her lap. "What do you want me to autograph?"

He rummaged in his pocket and pulled out a small leather-bound notebook. He flicked through a number of pages with scrawl on them until he found a blank sheet. "Here, please, if you will."

* * *

Fireman Glen O'Berne was sweating, having shoveled about two tons of coal in less than half an hour. He was just finishing spreading the coal through the open firehole door, from front to back and into the corners to keep the furnace hot.

Charlie Van Horn, the engineer, sat on the right, a hand idling on the emergency brake wheel. He eyed the boiler pressure gauge. "That'll do nicely, Glen," he bellowed.

With a thick oily rag wrapped round his hand, Glen grabbed the fire door handle and shut off the fire hole.

"Get up there on your seat and sit yourself down," Charlie said. "And afore ye do, best crack open your door and let's have a smoke."

"There'll be no smoking for now." A man called from the top of the stacked coal in the tender. His Colt was leveled on Glen.

"What in tarnation is this?" Charlie snarled.

"Just keep your hands where I can see them. It's a hold up, that's what it is. Carry on as you're doing." Awkwardly, the man slid off the heap of coal, dislodging some chunks that clattered on the ridged iron plate at the engineer's feet. He steadied himself holding a metal strut. He held out a sheet of paper with the track drawn on it, the place marked with an 'X.' "When you get here, you're going to go into reverse."

"Like hell I will!"

The outlaw fired, the bullet missing Charlie and the brake pressure gauge by inches, zinging off metal. The shot was drowned by the sound of the locomotive. "I can drive this thing if I must, fella. If I have to, I will, but I'm not keen on shooting you both, since I'd rather let you do the work." He shrugged. "Your choice."

Charlie snatched the sheet of paper from him. "All right, dammit. Just don't go shooting up my cab anymore."

CHAPTER 4

Everyone's a Critic

The first inkling Carter had that something was wrong came when he felt the train begin to brake and slow down. He had memorized the map in preparation for this assignment. At less than an hour after embarkation, nothing much existed in this stretch of land. That the train was slowing meant trouble.

His hunch was confirmed when the rear door of the salon car swung open and a man entered, boldly stating, "You're all my captives, folks." He was stocky, broad-shouldered and unusually dressed for an outlaw, wearing a pin-stripe suit, vest, and a brown derby hat. He wore a double holster and belt in tooled leather carrying two Smith & Wesson .45s.

"Who the hell are you?" demanded Mr. Halsworth, rising from his armchair.

"My name is Sid Banning." He waved the two .45s in emphasis. "Remember it well. After today I'll be more famous than Jesse James or Sam Bass." He was speedily flanked by three other armed men, who moved among the seated passengers. The door slammed shut after them.

Varying degrees of consternation appeared on the faces of those present. Carter noticed the senator's daughter raised a hand to her mouth. Gebhard placed a hand over Lillie's, the actress having the presence of mind to put a finger in her book to keep her place. Sykes scowled, his brow wrinkling. The politicians leaned forward in their seats but didn't get up. Newsman Emerson's eyes widened, as if in recognition—maybe he'd seen a wanted dodger for Banning before. Holtman downed his drink in a nervous gulp.

"Everybody sit tight," Banning ordered.

The number of people who knew Carter's status as a detective remained low on purpose. If nothing happened during the trip, the passengers in the salon car would think he was merely an actor. If something did happen, he would play his cards close to the vest and see what he could accomplish.

He kept his badge in a small pouch on the inside of his belt. It was easily retrieved but not easily discovered when searched. It wouldn't do any good to be found out as a lawman so early in this takeover, especially when there were four outlaws wielding guns.

Halsworth, however, had other ideas. Being one of the few men who knew Carter's identity, he gave the detective an imploring eye. It was as if the older man was pleading for Carter to do something. The detective dared not react for fear of giving himself away. The odds were four-to-one here, and Carter knew there must be others. It was only when he saw Halsworth open his mouth to speak that Carter's hand was forced.

With his heart slamming in his chest, improvising a foppish hero, Carter rose from his seat. "What is this all about?"

The burly outlaw in the gray coat who smelled more jackass than man swung his gun in Carter's direction. The butt slammed into Carter's chin. He saw stars and knew blood had been drawn. He stumbled to his knees on the carpet.

Carter's assailant waved his Colt. "Do as the boss tells you." He swung round, menacingly. "That means all of you."

"Go easy, Mule," Banning said, putting a restraining hand on the outlaw's arm.

Carter noticed Mule had a slate-colored eye. The left one was gray glass. His mind raced over the posted dodgers of known outlaws in the area. He came up blank.

"Remember, they're our captives," Banning berated. "We need them all in one piece—for now, at least."

His allusion to "for now" evinced a shocked intake of breath from quite a few.

There followed a lot of grumbling and murmuring, but nobody else appeared to want to start a fight or speak out.

Docilely, Carter clambered back into his armchair.

One of the men moved swiftly over to the bar and covered the barkeep and the two newsmen. The rest spread out, guns drawn, watchful.

The train, having ground to a halt, shuddered a moment. Then, with a whistle of steam and a great lurch, the locomotive began to move again.

In reverse.

Banning grinned at the captives, clearly relishing their confused faces. "We're going to search each of you. If you're carrying weapons, I'd advise you to show them— slowly—and we'll kindly take them off your hands." He laughed. "It's for your own good. Dangerous things, pea shooters."

Carter dabbed his chin with his linen handkerchief. The blood had quickly dried and crusted, but he repeated the agitated motion. He even ground the cloth into his bruised chin to better evoke pain. The result each time was that the scab opened, and he started bleeding once more. It was his personal retribution for missing his opportunity to prevent the commandeering.

"We'll start with you, Mr. Hero," Banning said, pointing his gun at Carter.

In his time in the theater, Carter had met a few magicians. A key feature to all good magic tricks was sleight of hand and making sure an audience saw what the magician wanted them to see, which meant they didn't see the magician's other hand.

With a flourish, Carter opened his jacket, revealing his shoulder holster. Banning cocked his head, his brows furrowing slightly, almost like he was impressed.

"What kind of man carries a gun no one can see?" Banning asked.

Shrugging, Carter said, "One who doesn't like wrinkles in his suit." He cocked an eyebrow, allowing his eyes to travel up and down Banning's clothes, clearly indicating all the wrinkles on the outlaw's own duds.

Carter's revolver was tugged out of his shoulder holster by the beefy hands of a brute of a man who answered to the moniker Karl. This one Carter recognized. He had a $4,000 reward on his head, dead or alive. Karl was wanted for rape and murder. He still had the bushy brown beard, moustache, and eyebrows depicted in the poster, and now a smouldering stogie was lodged in the corner of his mouth. But Karl didn't find the derringer in Carter's left boot or the knife in his right. Sadly, that little pistol wasn't going to provide sufficient threat or firepower to take back control of the train. Yet he hoped it might prove useful at some opportune moment.

Banning holstered his pistols. He stood in front of Jessica who sat rigid in her chair. "Stand up, miss."

She stood in compliance.

He snatched her small purse and emptied its belongings on the floor. There was nothing of intrinsic value, and he swept away the contents with his boot. Dropping the purse, he moved closer, and his hands slid inside her bolero jacket. They came away empty. Her high cheekbones were flush, and her lower lip trembled. And then he stroked her waist and hips, salaciously yet quite perfunctorily. "Okay, sit."

She sat, tight-lipped, grim-faced.

Banning walked over to Lillie Langtry. "Stand, if you please, ma'am."

She unfolded gracefully from her armchair. "Since you ask so courteously." She then emptied her purse onto the carpet, dropped it and stood with her hands on her hips.

His eyes on her, menacingly, he moved closer. "Are you hiding something else?" Suddenly, his hands groped at her green silk bodice.

Her face transformed into a fiery red shade and she backed off a step, manicured hand slapping his cheek resoundingly hard.

A couple of Banning's men laughed.

He slapped her face in return and she staggered a pace backward.

Gebhard lunged from his seat to aid Lillie but Banning's fist quickly knocked the manager to the carpeted floor.

Simultaneously, Carter darted from his seat and punched Banning on the back of his neck, sending the owlhoot sprawling into the arms of two of his men. Carter had been about to draw his derringer from his boot when Mule hit him on his much-abused chin with what felt like a sledgehammer. Carter slumped to the floor and, within the blink of an eye, he was staring into the snout of Mule's six-gun.

"Stop!" Banning growled, steadying himself.

Banning glowered down at Carter and rubbed the back of his neck. "We already decided who," he paused, as if searching for the right word, "to let off the train first." He grinned and ugly yellow teeth festered behind cracked lips. "But, since our unsuspecting patrons probably won't pay right away," he said, pointing at Carter, "you'll be next as an incentive."

With that promise, Mule's aimed pistol moved away from Carter's head and then it exploded, the shot fired directly at Roger Halsworth. Carter winced at the close loud crash of noise and his stomach wrenched in sympathy, for he could see that the gut shot had doubled Halsworth over. Then the executive collapsed to the floor.

"Time for a delivery," Banning said.

He and all the other desperados laughed uproariously.

With deliberate slowness, Banning pulled an envelope from his inside pocket and pierced a hole in it with a knife. Then he fastened a leather cinch through the hole and around Halsworth's neck. In response, the executive moaned.

Banning signaled to two men. "Abe, Mule, take him to the boxcar. You know what to do."

"Will do, Boss." Obediently, the pair stooped, lifted up the moaning executive and part carried, part dragged him out the rear door of the car, heading toward the center of the train.

Minutes later, through the window Carter glimpsed Halsworth's body flying out onto a station platform which they were racing past.

"Gentlemen and ladies, we have just delivered an ultimatum," Banning said. "If our demands are not met by sunset today, then we start eliminating one of you each hour until the authorities finally see sense and comply with our requirements."

"That's horrendous!" Jessica exclaimed, her whole body trembling.

"Young lady, nobody else needs to die if our demands are met. And you, of all people, should understand that."

A short while after they'd got rid of Halsworth, Carter glanced around the salon car to gauge how his fellow captives were handling the situation. To his right sat the two women. Lillie Langtry, her face still marked with the handprint of Banning's slap, held her head high and looked straight ahead, out the window. Gebhard patted her hand, but she seemed to ignore the gesture.

Halsworth's bloodstain was illuminated by the sun streaming in through the skylight. The politicians peered at the rug, but they didn't linger, shying away from the blemish as if it might contaminate them. The newsmen, having identified themselves and their profession to Banning, furiously scribbled in their notebooks. With Banning's desire for notoriety, he happily allowed Emerson and Holtman to record the event for posterity.

Carter knew none of these men could be counted on to help him retake the train. It would seem he had until sunset, if nothing transpired, to free them before his turn—the "next time." Somehow, that wasn't a comforting thought.

That left, Carter realized, only one alternative. He was going to have to do something. And he was going to have to do it alone, even if with only a derringer and a knife.

CHAPTER 5

Naked Blade

It was a tense waiting game and the waiting always got Karl Wilde on edge. Worse, it was stifling with so many bodies in the salon car. He needed to get away. In fact, he had an almost overpowering urge to spill blood.

Banning laid out strict orders for the barkeep, only two shots of liquor for each of his men, no more. The barkeep complied, pouring with a shaky hand, and inevitably spilling some on the counter.

"Hey, don't waste it!" the outlaw growled, which only made the man tremble harder.

"Free drinks, eh?" said Karl as he sidled up to Banning. The cigar between his lips bobbed as he lit it.

"Yup, on the house," Banning replied, drolly. "I'll get us food later. It's gonna be a long day."

"I reckon you're right." Karl paused. "Say, Boss, since everything's in hand here, I was thinking I could go to the back and help sort through the passengers' valuables."

"Yeah, that'll be fine. Hey, check on the brothers in the boxcar, in case they need some assistance, too."

"Sure thing, Boss."

"Don't take all day, though. I want you back here soon."

Nodding, Karl made his way to the rear of the car. He grinned at Mule who stepped aside for him to exit.

The rush of air was a big relief. He'd gotten away, if only for a short while. Karl felt the blood in his body run faster in anticipation.

The first compartment he came upon held the men who were trussed and gagged, just as he and the others had left them. One by one, he hauled them to their feet and shoved them out into the corridor, amid muffled objections. "This room'll be occupied soon," he said, puffing on the cigar.

Karl balled up his fists to prod the men down the corridor until they came to the next compartment. Inside were several other men and an elderly woman, also tied and gagged. "Folks, you've got company," he said, motioning the men he was escorting to join the others. He slammed the door shut. It was sure going to get hot and sweaty in there, but he didn't care.

Smoking the stogie, he continued on his way to the next car, checking each compartment as he passed. He got a thrill at the look of pure terror in the eyes of all the incapacitated passengers. One was a middle-aged woman who had caught his eye while everyone was boarding, but she wasn't the one he was looking for.

He crossed into the next car and stopped at the second compartment. Four men and two women sat with their hands tied behind their backs. Their eyes lanced at him.

The man nearest the door managed to quickly work his gag loose. In a croaking voice, he said, "What do you want now? You've got everything!"

Karl's eyes landed on the redheaded woman. His lips curled away from his teeth. "Not everything." He pointed at her. "You're coming with me."

She shook her head adamantly while sinking further into her seat.

Karl leaned in, grabbed her arm, and hauled her to her feet.

"You swine," the man yelled, "leave her be!"

Viciously, Karl planted a fist in the man's face to shut him up.

While the others squirmed and made stifled, alarmed noises, Karl pulled the woman out into the corridor and slammed the door shut.

Brutishly, he shoved her ahead of him along the swaying hall.

When they got to the interconnecting doors, he grabbed the rope that tethered her wrists. "Don't get any ideas about jumping off, honey. I'll be keeping a tight rein on you."

She walked the rest of the way ahead of him until he pushed her into the empty compartment, and she dropped to the floor.

He took out his knife, and as he moved closer, she closed her eyes tight.

Chewing on his cigar, he cut into the front of her jacket. She shuddered at the sound of slicing of the fabric and jerked backward when the knife nicked the skin of her neck.

"You don't cry, huh?" Karl said.

She shook her head with a determined grit.

"I'll remove that gag so long as you keep quiet. One peep and I'll knock you cold," he said, then slowly removed the gag to let her speak.

"Mister, I won't give you the gratification."

Karl sneered and replaced the gag. He raised the knife again, then began cutting her blouse and corset when he heard voices in the corridor. He quickly went to the door and listened. The distinctive Arkansas drawls meant it had to be the Yates brothers. Karl figured they must have finished in the boxcar with the mail, faster than he'd expected. Maybe they weren't simpletons after all.

After the brothers had passed by, Karl swore under his breath, then pointed at the redhead with a feral streak in his eyes. "I'll be back, honey, I promise."

She writhed against the restraints holding her arms back as he left the compartment and slammed the door shut.

CHAPTER 6

Invisibility

Early afternoon

Colonel Furlow had the lead to the mysterious Area 53 with Miles and Cash closely following. The route twisted along a wide mountain incline, a seemingly much used route flattened by countless wheels. The horses stirred up dust that swirled and blew away on the breeze.

Eventually, they rode up to a sturdy wooden gate guarded by two armed troopers and a high barbed wire fence that stretched for at least a couple hundred yards on either side of the gate and then continued on around.

A sergeant stepped forward and saluted. "Colonel, sir! Welcome back. They're expecting you at the farmhouse."

"Good to hear, Sergeant Aikens."

The soldier waved to the other guard who opened the gate.

They rode through and covered about half a mile of an upgrade, before coming to a mountain meadow. At the far end was another gate and fence, and beyond it was an immense building with an unusual roof structure attached to pulleys and derricks.

They were waved through the gate without hindrance or comment.

As they rode nearer, Cash peered up at what was more warehouse than farmhouse. The odd roof was at least four stories high. The two marshals exchanged a look. Cash raised an eyebrow. "What the hell?"

"Professor Blaylock is, um, eccentric," Furlow said. He tied his horse to the hitching post outside the 'farmhouse,' well-guarded by troopers armed with carbines.

Cash and Miles left their mounts and stayed on the colonel's heels, going up a couple of steps to a door manned by two uniformed soldiers. A corporal held a logbook while the other, a private, held a rifle in readiness.

Furlow handed over his credentials. The corporal checked his book, returned the papers, and saluted. He motioned to the private who, with some difficulty, opened the right-hand side of an oversized double door.

The three men went into the mostly empty building which appeared even more enormous than from the outside.

A sentry jolted out of his chair, stood to attention and saluted the colonel. "Sir!"

"At ease, son."

Workbenches lined the walls with various tools spread out. Three large wood and metal tanks stood on one side, with copper plumbing snaking out of them. "They're the generators," Furlow said. "Filled with sulphuric acid and iron filings to produce hydrogen gas."

Cash nodded, none the wiser. He looked at a series of cables that were anchored to the floor by heavy ring bolts spaced every 10 to 15 feet in a large oval. What awed and puzzled him at the same time was when he followed the cables upward, they appeared to be hanging in mid-air at the far end.

He thought the cables resembled the ropes he'd seen for a ship at harbor, but these led nowhere.

Furlow looked left and right, spinning in a circle. He turned to the guard standing at ease. "The telegraph message said we were to meet the Professor here."

"And so you will," a voice thundered from thin air.

Both Cash and Miles looked but saw no one else around.

The disembodied voice continued. "Why is the military meddling in my work again, Colonel?" Cash felt sure it had come from the vacant space in the middle of the cables.

"Professor," Furlow said, his tone bordering on irate, "if you would show yourself, I would like to introduce you."

"Blast it!" the professor exclaimed.

Cash heard a cranking sound, and slowly, suspended from above, a man appeared turning a handle. Then he disappeared just as quickly.

"Gentlemen," Furlow said, extending his hand upward, as if he were the ringmaster in a circus, "I present to you, *The Pegasus*."

As Cash and Miles gazed up in wonderment as the huge, floating ship materialized into view.

"Here it is, no longer in its cloaked mode," Furlow said.

"Quite a trick to hide such a huge thing," Miles said.

"I've never seen its like before," Cash said. "I've seen pictures in the *Illustrated Newspaper* of the observation balloons used in the Civil War, but those were tiny by comparison."

The Pegasus was gigantic, the length of two Mississippi River steamboats end to end. The craft's wooden exterior was rounded both fore and aft. It reminded Cash of a U.S. naval frigate complete with a large steering wheel aft of the ship and a figurehead in the shape of a horse's head at the bow. In the forebody of the ship, glass windows with brass fittings allowed passengers to look down on the earth while aloft.

Long, sturdy wings extended out from each side of the airship. The tradesmen took an obvious pride in the design because the underside of each wing was carved to resemble bird feathers—perhaps to confound observers on terra firma who happened to catch sight of it when visible.

Surrounding the entire structure was a latticework of iron and wood, all separated into squares roughly a yard across. Within each square, a pane of glass was positioned on a central rod. Cranks adjacent to the steering wheel rotated the panes of glass out and in. In its cloaked form, all the panes rested within each frame, and a series of mirrors reflected the image from above the ship. The end result, inside the hanger, was that *The Pegasus* reflected the ceiling of the building.

Cash smiled as he realized what had drawn his attention. The ceiling of this cavernous place was buttressed by mighty pillars of wood extending across the entire roof. When he first looked up, the cross-hatched pattern looked off. This would not be a problem when it came to blue skies or clouds. There was no frame of reference when an onlooker gazed up from the ground. The effect would render *The Pegasus* completely invisible, even in plain sight.

"I can't believe what I'm seeing," Miles said. "Or not seeing!"

"It has to be tremendously heavy. How does it stay in the air?" Cash asked.

Furlow explained, "*The Pegasus* is essentially hollow. All except for the engines and balloon that's inside. The *exoskeleton*, as the professor calls it, provides the framework to attach the mirrors that hide the airship and provides protection. The wings are for balance. If necessary, there are emergency balloons that can be inflated using onboard steam engines."

"How is it propelled?" Cash wondered.

"The same steam engines that keep the balloon inflated also power the working propeller in the aft," Furlow replied. "That would be the rear."

While Colonel Furlow talked, the airship shimmered and gradually vanished again. A square hole appeared above, and a rope ladder dropped. A man dressed in a brown chalk-stripe suit and vest, red suspenders, and black lace-up shoes descended the ladder that, from the group's angle, seemed to be dangling in thin air. Once on firm ground, he turned to face the three of them.

"Professor Quinten Blaylock," said Furlow, motioning to the man.

Blaylock looked to be in his early fifties with a monocle scrunched in his right eye socket. He had shaggy brown eyebrows and tufts of hair sprouted from his ears. His hair was just as bushy but graying slightly. A perplexity of anger corrugated the skin around his light brown eyes. He was average height but unusually thin and his hawk-like way of slouching made him appear taller than he was actually. "So

Colonel," he said, his voice grating and high-pitched, "I am told that my airship is to be used for a preposterous rescue mission?"

Furlow offered a long-suffering smile. "Now Professor, you know the Department of War is footing the bill for your project and can use it as they see fit. The rescuing of so many important people will be viewed favorably by President McKinley and likely to benefit your future funding. He is, after all, supportive of scientific advances."

Beads of sweat collected in Blaylock's brows. His unblinking gaze met Furlow's eyes. "Bah, he is a nincompoop just like all politicians. Did you know that former President Harrison and his wife wouldn't even touch light switches for fear of getting an electric shock? They were even reported to go to sleep with the lights on because of their imbecilic anxiety. How ludicrous. Who knows what that overgrown walrus of an ex-lawyer Cleveland believed, but I don't give a damn—"

"Now, now, Professor, this is a humanitarian mission and I plead to your sense of charity."

"Harrumph!" Blaylock removed the monocle from his eye and cleaned it with a yellow, linen handkerchief.

Cash hid a grin. He found it ironic that Furlow himself had resorted to Blaylock's argument just a few hours before.

Furlow proceeded to introduce Miles and Cash.

The professor replaced the monocle and looked from marshal to marshal, studying them from head to toe.

He opened his mouth to say something just as Senator Madison arrived with a contingent of armed troopers. "I see we're in time, Colonel," said the senator. He stood and gaped at the dangling rope ladder, raised his black homburg hat and scratched his forehead. "My God, you told me about the invisibility, but seeing the effect, it's incredible!" The newly arrived soldiers stared in disbelief. "Are you sure you have room for all of us, Professor?"

"It will be crowded, I grant you, as space is at a premium, but it is designed to hold up to fifty individuals." Blaylock eyed the soldiers. "All of you just be sure to fasten your restraints and keep them clasped while we're aloft." He turned on his heel abruptly and headed back to the rope ladder. Holding onto a rung, he said, "I'm taking off in an hour."

"Better make that two," Furlow countered. "We need to go over the maps of the terrain."

Blaylock arched a brow over his good eye and offered a mischievous grin. "Colonel, when I fly and see the land below me, I don't need maps."

CHAPTER 7

Won the Privilege

Late afternoon

As the day wore on, a pattern emerged. The *Sundown Express* traveled over a certain section of land. After about an hour, the train would come to a halt. Then, in rapid fashion, it would start up again in the opposite direction. Each time the train reversed course, the bandits in the salon car stationed themselves at either end, rifles and six shooters at the ready in case someone on the ground tried to take the train. Only Banning remained calm and inside the salon. He carried himself almost with an air of invincibility and calmness, secure in the thought he had planned out every detail.

The passengers, on the other hand, were far from calm. Anxiety hovered in the air. Conversation was stilted, for fear, left unvoiced, gnawed at every thought. Carter stared out the window and sifted through everything up until that moment. One thing that bedeviled his thoughts was the vetting process. How had Banning and his gang gained access to the train? The more he thought about it, the more he arrived at the only logical conclusion. Yet he was pretty sure he'd not have a chance to discover the truth, not without exposing himself as a detective. Granted, he was already on Banning's short list. When the outlaw leader came next for Carter, the detective wondered how he would get the upper hand. Unfortunately, unlike a bad poker hand, if Carter folded now, it meant his death. He had to change the odds.

Carter straightened up in his seat as the door at the front of the luxury salon car opened. The sentry stepped to one side and Banning strode in, then Karl, and trailing behind him, two fellow outlaws, White with his unkempt whiskers and swarthy complexion and Greene who sported a crooked nose and coal-besmirched clothes. All four seemed cheerful, joshing in low voices, their cheeks slightly flushed.

Much earlier, Carter had overheard their names, though he didn't know how useful that might be. By all accounts, outlaws changed their names more often than they changed their socks. A tall guy with ash-blond hair answered to the name of Abe Stone. He stood out from the others, sporting an embroidered buckskin shirt with fringe trim, corduroy pants and tooled leather boots. Alongside him was Morgan Miller, a good six inches shorter than Stone, with hazel-green eyes and coal black hair. His trail-worn blue shirt and brown vest were criss-crossed with bandoliers of shells. A Bowie knife hung from his belt, and he gripped a Winchester '73. Both were likely in their mid-to-late twenties. Wasting their youth in the pursuit of easy riches.

It seemed an age ago when they had passed through a tunnel, the lighting in the car subdued, shadows abounding. When they emerged, two other men had appeared from the rear of the train, and he learned they were the Yates brothers though they could have sprung from different mothers. Both in their early-twenties, Teddy was fat with a beer keg belly and tended to bully his sibling, while Toby was thin and lanky with a receding jaw. In this heat, Teddy must have been uncomfortable wearing a heavy button-down plaid wool shirt, even if it was open at the neck, for there was also a glimpse underneath of a red union suit. Toby was more sensible, in denim jacket and pants.

Another man, Mule Dunn, stood by the door at the other end of the carriage, eyeing the captives, a hand resting on the butt of his holstered revolver, as if daring someone to try something.

The captives watched, tension etched in their faces, as the four men stopped and stood in front of Jessica Madison and Lillie Langtry who were seated next to each other.

Banning toed Jessica's black ankle boot.

Boldly, she looked up. Her gaze lingered on Stone for a moment and then leveled on Banning.

Shrugging, Banning said, "Sorry, Miss Madison."

Her lips trembled and it appeared she wanted to ask what he meant by apologizing. Then she got her answer as Banning turned to Karl standing at his shoulder.

"Okay, Karl," Banning said to the big ugly brute. "You drew the best card and won the privilege."

"That's the 'Wilde' luck," Karl leered, relishing in the thought that he now had the senator's daughter in addition to the redhead.

Abe Stone stepped forward. "Boss, it ain't right. We came for the money." He gestured vaguely at Jessica. "Not this."

Karl chortled. "Speak for yourself, kid." He shoved Abe aside and moved closer to Lillie and Jessica. His large, beefy hand shot out and grabbed Jessica's thin arm, and he pulled her to her feet.

Jessica flinched as he leaned close, breathing heavily over her.

Abe grabbed Karl's arm and tugged.

Without faltering, Karl drew his six-gun and slammed the barrel against Abe's chin, breaking the skin. Abe stumbled backward, with White catching him before he fell.

Abe wiped the blood from his chin and Carter felt a rueful twinge of empathy.

"Don't interfere, kid," Karl snarled, "or I'll make sure your face don't look so pretty anymore."

"Easy, now," Banning barked. "I won't have y'all bustin' each other up."

Abe shrugged his shoulders and scowled, his blue eyes baleful.

"Abe, go to the rear, stay with Zeke, out of trouble."

Reluctantly, Abe nodded. At the door, he cast an anxious look at Jessica before he left.

Banning laid a hand on Karl's shoulder. "You too, Karl. We don't need any fighting among ourselves."

"Sorry, Boss. I got excited, is all."

"All right, just take it down a peg, you hear?"

Karl nodded and turned to Jessica, still holding her tight. "Let's you and me go get acquainted, honey."

Undaunted by their display of aggression, Lillie stood and tried to pry Karl away from Jessica. "Unhand her, you animal!"

Carter admired her pluck but she might as well have been trying to move the trunk of a redwood.

Karl simply laughed.

She let go, stepped back, and spread her arms wide in front of her. "If you want someone, take me." Her eyes were as cold as ice while a red-hot flush rose to her cheeks. "Just leave her be."

Karl licked his lips and glanced questioningly at Banning.

Eyes wide, Banning said, "Such a gallant gesture, Miss Langtry. I praise your courage." He looked around at the captives. "You've got more sand than all these men here, that's for sure." He grinned at her. "Don't worry. Your turn's coming." He gritted his teeth and leaned close to her, almost nose-to-nose. "Now *sit!*"

Lillie's face seethed but, knowing she was outpowered, she dropped into her seat, hunching herself as far away from Karl and Banning as possible. She looked up at Jessica with apologies in her eyes.

"Now with that settled, take her outta here, Karl," Banning said, slapping Jessica's butt.

Banning's gang laughed crudely.

Jessica dug in her heels as Karl shoved her across the car.

Holding her by the neck, he waited while Mule opened the back door and then pushed her out.

The sudden surge of air and the sound of the train pounding the rails drowned out her plaintive cries for help.

CHAPTER 8

Goldbeater's Skin

The Pegasus strained at its moorings while a number of troopers worked at windlasses placed around the building. Slowly, gradually, the pulleys heaved sections of the roof up until it was fully open to the sky.

"Cast off!" ordered the professor from his position at the forepeak of the airship. His monocle stashed in a breast pocket, Blaylock now sported leather-and-glass goggles.

With military precision, the mooring ropes were unloosed.

At first, Cash experienced queasiness in the pit of his stomach as the craft rose into the air.

Behind Professor Blaylock, standing but safely strapped to struts were Colonel Furlow in his uniform, complete with saber in its scabbard, Cash, Miles, Senator Madison, and twenty troopers armed with Springfield carbines. The soldiers wore strapped-down forage caps. The colonel had left his hat behind. Cash and Miles did the same, also stowing their spurs in their saddlebags before departure. "Neither is going to be much use scrambling down a rock chimney," Cash had observed.

The central walkway of wooden slats had a hatch in the middle. On the wall to the left, a rope ladder was stowed. Levers, knobs, and gauges littered the console and metal pipes snaked along the wood walls toward the rear where the steam engine churned and the two-man crew worked in synchronicity.

It was strange being encased by hundreds of mirrors and not being able to see anything outside the aircraft. The professor had been adamant, however, the craft would maintain its invisibility as soon as it was launched. He had no wish to disclose its secretive presence.

To navigate and steer, the professor had rigged up a number of internal wide-angle mirrors that pointed through tiny gaps between external mirrors and revealed to him the countryside ahead and below without exposing the interior of the exoskeleton with its passengers, crew, steam engines, and other equipment.

He was proud of his vessel. "A hundred years ago, balloons could only manage flights of a very limited duration," he explained. "At that time, small balloons were made of varnished silk, and after that they used varnished linen. But, you see, the hydrogen gas has the smallest molecule of all the elements so it tends to leak through most materials."

Cash looked anxiously at the patchwork walls within their exoskeleton.

"Six or so years ago," the professor went on, "I began to use goldbeater's skin, as it's almost completely impermeable."

"Goldbeater's skin?" Miles queried.

"From the production of gold leaf. Very thin, very fine."

"Sounds expensive," said Cash.

"It is, but the government can afford it. The outer layer of the large intestine of cattle and thin pieces of gold are interleaved and beaten until very thin. Fortunately, our country is blessed with countless cattle, as we do require thousands. You see, the skin is only available in small pieces so has to be joined together to make sheets large enough for a balloon gas cell. Several layers are required."

Cash thought of balloons as being quiet. But this was a noisy contraption, for sure.

A stoker fed a small furnace near the rear, to generate the steam and operate the propellers. According to the professor, once airborne, the craft didn't require a great deal of power to move.

"How fast can you travel in this…?" Cash asked, biting back the word *contraption*.

"Easily as fast as the train, even faster. At some point, I will need to match *The Pegasus*'s speed to that of the train."

"But then how will you stop over the hole in the rock to lower us?" Miles queried.

"It hovers well, have no worries. I simply disengage the propellers a few seconds beforehand."

"What about wind, drift in the air?" the colonel pressed.

Blaylock tapped six leather handles sticking out of the left-hand console. "These extra little levers can operate small vents on either side. They expel small spurts of steam to adjust the airship's position. Long enough to maintain position while we lower you all."

"It sounds foolproof," said Miles, his tone unconvinced.

"Science doesn't allow for fools, but there is always room for imponderables. Any scientist worth his weight surely will account for this, which is why rigorous practice and testing is a must in order to achieve reproducible and reliable technological advancement."

"So how often have you practiced and tested for this jaunt?" Cash asked.

"Oh, this will be the first attempt. But the principles are sound."

"That's real comforting," Miles said.

* * *

"Sonovabitch!" Feeling suppressed fury, like heat radiating off a branding iron, Abe crossed the gap between the salon and the compartment cars. He knew of Karl's reputation with women, and he shuddered at the thought of what he might do to Jessica Madison, given half a chance.

He was just passing the first compartment when one of the blinds rolled up with a loud clatter. He started at the sound. And then he gasped.

A young, redheaded woman in ripped clothing was standing wide-eyed in the center of the room, bleeding from a cut on her neck. She must have kicked at the blinds, loosening one.

"Sick bastard!" he said, knowing it had to be Karl's doing. The boss would explode when he found out that Karl was going out on his own.

I can't leave her here.

Sliding the door open, he slipped inside, and closed the blinds. She recoiled, fear etched on her face.

"Hey," he said soothingly, "I'm not going to hurt you. I'm gonna get you outta here. Take you back to your compartment. I know which one."

She warily allowed him to approach and wrap an arm around her waist for support.

He checked that the corridor was clear, then helped her back to her friends who were relieved to see her.

Making his way to the rear of the train to join Zeke, just as Banning had ordered, he smirked at the thought of Karl returning to the compartment where he'd left his captive and finding it empty.

* * *

Vincenzi, one of the politicians, rose from his chair and stepped forward. "Now, see here, you…"

A mite late, Carter thought. Vincenzi's intervention would have been more fitting if he'd come forward while Jessica was still here to be liberated.

Without warning, Banning spun round and pummeled Vincenzi in his considerable gut.

The politician doubled over, crashing to the floor and fell upon the bloodstain left by Halsworth. He lay, gasping for breath, a crimson sheen across one side of his face.

"Any more heroes?" Banning called out, a hand massaging his fist.

Carter stood. "Just me." Ice traced his spine. He was acting a fool, but he had no option.

Banning turned, a grin cracking his weathered face. "Oh, Dandy Boy. You're speaking out of turn again. You *can't* be a hero. You're our next messenger." He gave a signal and two of the outlaws—Mule and White—closed in.

Clicking his fingers, Banning said, "That reminds me, it's time for another special delivery."

"Hey," Carter said, "I thought you weren't going to kill any more captives until sunset?"

"This is my train. My rules. I can change my mind when I want. I reckon they need an occasional reminder to hurry and get that money ready."

"It takes time to count all those greenbacks," Carter offered in mitigation.

"You don't understand the fine art of negotiating," Banning chided. "Reminders let them know we mean business."

Carter held up a hand. "I don't mind dying," he said, adding under his breath, "I've done it more than once before." His mind raced, trying to find some means to stall the inevitable. He looked around. Not the ideal audience for a final curtain. The two bandits now flanked him, each grabbing an arm. Their grips were akin to vices. Carter winced.

"Not so tight, gentlemen. You'll stop the blood flow."

In response, Mule and White tightened their fists.

Carter winced again, this time, much more exaggerated. "It's just…" He trailed off and looked at the faces of the other captives. Important men, rich men, some staring at him, others averting their eyes in guilty knowledge of their own cowardice.

And there was Lillie Langtry, beautiful as ever, even if the lines around her eyes betrayed her fear.

"Yes?" Banning said.

Slowly, Carter turned and faced Banning. He let the grin creep across his face until he felt it imbue his entire body with projected confidence.

"If you want to live, let me tell you about your three mistakes."

CHAPTER 9

Blood That's Due

"We're getting close!" Blaylock shouted. "Open the hatch!"

Cash unlatched the access and lifted it. Peering through goggles, he blinked. The ground was rushing beneath them at a rapid pace. He leaned forward, ducking his head through the hole. "There's the *Sundown Express*," he said, pointing to the train that was no more than a series of dots below. His hair blew in the wind whipping across the bow of *The Pegasus*.

"The mountain's near," Blaylock said. "We're ahead of the train."

"Professor," Cash said, "if we're going to do this, we need to be in place by the time the *Express* enters the tunnel."

"Agreed. I'll navigate the airship to the top aperture so your party can descend before the train even enters." Blaylock grinned and adjusted his goggles. "Lower the ladder and head on down. Leave the piloting to me."

Miles dropped the ladder through the hatch and moved to the side, offering Cash first place in line. Colonel Furlow mustered up close behind Miles.

The nearest trooper looked at the three men preparing to depart and remarked, "I'm sure glad the rest of us don't have to go down there with you."

* * *

Banning sneered through gritted teeth. "Dandy, I don't make mistakes."

Carter fought not to wince as the two men tightly gripped his arms. "Well, you did this time. Your first mistake was not having the *Sundown Express* stop at any station. How are you going to know if the ransom is to be paid? How are you to know you don't need to kill me?"

Pursing his lips, Banning said, "I have men at the fueling station. When we stop there to take on water and coal,"—he slipped his watch out of his vest pocket and checked the time—"in fifteen minutes, the men will tell me if our demands have been met." He pointed out the window. "Telegraph lines go to the station." He cocked his head. "You're just trying to weasel yourself out of a pine box."

Carter flexed his fingers, trying to keep the blood flowing. "I'll concede the point. But your second mistake was all of us." He indicated the somber captives standing behind Banning and his men.

"As soon as this little adventure of yours is over," Carter continued, gaining some strength in his voice, "we're all going to be able to identify your faces." He glanced back at his fellow prisoners but was chagrined to see only one man, the politician Allbeury no less, nod in agreement. "There won't be a bounty hunter alive that would scoff at the price put on your heads."

"Won't be a problem for you." Banning chuckled. He seemed to be enjoying the cat to mouse banter.

Carter pursed his lips. "Maybe not for me. But how long do you think you can live on the run, always looking over your shoulder? Besides, what's the alternative? Kill everyone here, leave no witnesses?" Light gasps escaped from some of the huddled captives.

"I say, steady there, Mr. Carter," Vincenzi expostulated breathlessly.

Ignoring him, Carter went on: "Believe me, in my line of work, there are always witnesses."

Banning moved forward, thrusting his face close to Carter's. "What's your line of work, anyway?"

Carter stood straighter, pushed out his chest, which was quite difficult with two owlhoots clamped onto his arms. "I'm an actor."

Banning and his men let out raucous laughter that filled the passenger car.

It was exactly what Carter wanted. "Your third mistake was..."

Banning grabbed Carter's shirt and drew him forward. The hands on his arms loosened. "Listen here, Mister Dandy Actor, my only mistake was letting you live this long." He signaled to two of his men. As they approached, he added, "The Yates brothers here, Teddy and Toby, like to hurt people. Do wicked things that I just as soon not see." He eyed Lillie briefly. "And we don't want to upset a proper actress, do we?"

Carter shook his head. "That's mighty considerate of you."

"I'm like that. So, the Yates boys are going to take you to the boxcar and make you wish you never boarded this train." He reached into his suit jacket, withdrew an envelope, and stuck it in the pocket of Carter's coat. "Then you're going to deliver the folks at the station another message."

Banning released his grip on Carter's shirt and punched him in the stomach.

Carter convulsed and went limp.

"That's to let you know this ain't no play you're in. It ain't make-believe. It's for real. Take him, lads."

* * *

Maintaining a strong grip on Jessica's arm, Karl pulled her across the gap between the salon and the compartment cars. "You're lucky. The boss wants you in one piece, more or less. But you'll get to see what will happen to you when we're finished here and have the money, for sure."

"When the authorities pay, you must let us go," she remonstrated over her shoulder.

He snorted. "Yeah, right. Get a move on!" He pushed her along the corridor.

She swung around and protested. "That was the deal. You can't cheat—"

"You're a mite simple, honey. We lie and cheat for a living. That's what outlaws do."

Her cheeks reddened. She flew at him, ankle-length boots kicking at his shins, her hands like claws attempting to scratch out his eyes. "You can't!"

Taken by surprise, he raised his arms in defense, backed off and tripped over his own feet. He landed on his ass on the floor, his left boot entangling in her skirt. Unbalanced,

Jessica tottered and fell, hitting her head against the corridor wall. She crumpled into a motionless lump.

Karl struggled to his knees and leaned over her. "You best be fine, or the boss will have my hide."

He inspected her head and found no blood, but a large bump was already forming on her forehead. Luckily, she was breathing alright.

Relieved all was not lost, he decided he could amuse himself with the redhead until this one regained consciousness. He got to his feet and lifted her in his arms.

Walking awkwardly in the confined corridor, he made for the first compartment.

Sliding the door open, he stumbled in the room, swaying with the motion of the train, carrying Jessica. He became immediately angered.

No redhead.

He swore and flung Jessica on the seat, then turned back to close the door behind him.

Not a moment too soon. He heard the Yates brothers again, this time they were manhandling someone. They must be taking the next victim to the boxcar. They passed the compartment and moved on, their voices diminishing and were soon gone.

Silence fell.

He glanced down at Jessica and felt powerful stirrings.

First things first.

CHAPTER 10

Headless

As the professor skillfully hovered *The Pegasus* over the shaft in the mountain, Cash clambered down the swaying ladder. Its swinging motion made his descent almost uncontrollable, especially as the weight and movement of Miles and the colonel were added. As his boots fumbled to find the next lower rung, he risked a glance above.

It was strange. From his vantage, it looked like the ladder snaked out from a hole in the sky. Colonel Furlow and Miles clung on, descending, as if they were part of a vaudeville illusion. There was no sign of the aircraft at all, save for the internal structure glimpsed in the square hatch.

He peered over his shoulder. Below, the train was approaching the tunnel mouth.

He hoped the engineer—or whoever was in charge of the loco—was intent on the rails ahead and not looking skyward. Still, if they were, it's likely they wouldn't believe their eyes.

Cash continued to descend the ladder whose end now extended far into the shaft in the rock.

"Precision timing, Professor," Cash said to himself.

Between the air-drift and the movement of the two men above him, Cash's shoulders occasionally, and painfully, buffeted the walls of the shaft as he persisted further down, it growing darker with each step.

He didn't know how far he'd gone. It struck him that he might have progressed past the end of the shaft and was now dangling into the tunnel, in which case the train would hit him at seventy miles per hour.

When a dim light appeared beneath his feet, Cash knew it must be the carbon arc lamp in front of the loco's smokestack, and it was casting just enough light for him to make out the lip of the shaft below. The ladder trailed about a foot further down, so he scaled the remaining rungs until his feet were level with the lip.

The thunderous sound was getting closer.

Abruptly, smoke and soot gushed up the shaft, choking him, as the engine passed underneath. He coughed, and let go of the ladder, falling through shaft to make way for the others, while there was still train to land on.

His boots hit the roof with a solid thud and his knees buckled as his feet were whipped from under him. He shouldn't have been surprised since he'd been virtually stationary while the surface he'd landed upon was moving exceedingly fast. He quickly crouched his body and clung to ridges on the roof surface. He was facing the rear of the train, the wind-rush battered his shoulders, threatening to dislodge him.

Internal lighting bounced off the tunnel walls but didn't illuminate the roof. He couldn't see clear enough to make out his partner or the colonel, so when he heard several faint clatterings, he assumed it to be Miles and Furlow landing on top of the train. He knew it would be pointless to shout, they would never hear him.

No sooner had the thought passed, daylight percolated from the tunnel mouth ahead.

Now he could actually see the shadowy shapes of the colonel and Miles atop different cars. The colonel had drawn his saber and was on the second-to-last car's roof, next to the caboose.

It wasn't the first time Cash had walked on the roof of a moving train, but he swore he'd never get used to it. Arms extended to either side, he regained his feet and staggered toward the rear. Miles was doing the same. He jumped the gap between two cars, landed unsteadily, but regained his footing and continued on. He remembered a time when he was in a stockyard and saw a brakeman on the snow-covered roof of a freight truck, working the handbrake, and then leaping to the next freight car to apply that brake, and so on. This was a cakewalk compared to that.

All three planned to meet at the rear of the caboose and then swing down, relying on surprise to confront any outlaws they'd find there. But the colonel hadn't waited for them. He'd swung down, out of sight.

An instant later, as Cash caught up and clapped a hand on Miles's shoulder, he saw a severed head fall away from the caboose and tumble along the track, swiftly disappearing in the darkness.

It wasn't Furlow's.

Cash signaled to Miles. They both leaned over the edge and swung down, placing their feet on the metal guardrail and then they jumped onto the rear coupling platform.

Colonel Furlow sat with his back against a wall, clasping his chest. The handle of a knife protruded. Blood slowly discolored the officer's uniform.

"He was quick," Furlow said. "But I was quicker." He coughed up blood.

"Keep still, Colonel," Cash said. "We'll get you help as soon as we can."

"I'm not going anywhere. You men go get 'em."

As Cash stepped over the headless corpse, he stooped down to remove a bandolier of shells that was wrapped round its chest, and then picked up the Winchester lying nearby. The colonel had killed silently, at any rate, so nobody in the next car was alerted.

Miles joined him, saying as quietly as possible, "The colonel ain't going to make it."

"I suppose not. Guess he thought he was above taking orders from civilians." Cash fastened the bandolier around his chest. Additional firepower was always welcome.

Miles pointed further back, in a shadowy corner. "There's the guardsman."

The man was dead, his throat cut, blood soaking the dapper clothing.

"Well, the poor bastard's been avenged," Cash opined.

They moved forward and stopped at the interconnecting door.

Cash ducked to the side of the window and peeked through. Across the gap between the cars, he could clearly see through the glass of the other car's door. About halfway down, two outlaws sat on either side of the aisle. One of them had the brim of his hat pulled low over his eyes, definitely asleep. The other, awake, his hogleg holstered, watched the passengers in their seats while rolling himself a cigarette.

"We can't start shooting. A lot of innocent people might get hurt or even killed."

"That's a tall order." Miles withdrew his knife. "But I can accommodate it."

Cash went back and picked up a black Stetson. "This must belong to the suddenly shortened guy." Fortunately, it wasn't bloody. He set it on his head. "Follow me in."

Miles nodded and crossed the open space and stood to one side on the small iron-plate platform, being careful to avoid being seen through the window.

Drawing his Colt, Cash turned the handle and slowly opened the door.

The wind and noise swishing past Cash and Miles alerted the awake outlaw, and he called over his shoulder, puffing on his cigarette. "Miller, why're you leavin' your post?"

Ignoring the concerned stares of several passengers cowering in their seats, Cash moved down the aisle, holding his six-gun behind him. Miles followed silently, knife ready.

As Cash closed in, the guy turned his head. "Hey, what the—" The man's eyes widened in astonishment. He anxiously reached across the aisle and tapped on his companion. "Zeke, Zeke!"

Cash swiftly pressed his Colt against the side of outlaw's neck and showed his badge, while Miles held his knife level on Zeke who was now roused.

Seeing the blade, Zeke sat very still, sweat sprouting on his forehead.

"It's almost a shame to wake Rip Van Winkle here," Miles said as he relieved Zeke of his six-gun.

"Miller jumped off," Cash advised Zeke's pal harshly.

Some of the passengers started talking, their voices rising in excitement.

Cash momentarily turned and raised a finger to his lips. "Quiet," he said, "we don't want the other outlaws put on guard." He flashed his badge to emphasize his authority. Their voices dropped to a murmur and then were silenced. Where there had seemed a heavy tension in the air when Cash and Miles entered the car, now there was a mood of subdued elation.

Eyeing the buckskin clad outlaw, Cash said, "What's your name, fella?"

"Abe Stone."

"Right, Abe, just answer my questions and you won't join Miller."

Abe gulped and nodded.

"Good man. Now, how many on board and where's the trail herder running your bunch?" Cash demanded.

Abe appeared reluctant to snitch on his pals, his chiseled face impassive, lips clamped together.

"Where?" Cash pressed the steel barrel against Abe's Adam's apple.

"There's two up front running the engine, Prout and Krebbs. Hoop's in the next car, and the Yates brothers are in the boxcar. Six more are in the lounge car with the bigwigs."

The muscles in Zeke's throat tightened and he seethed under his breath, "You blabbermouth."

"And your boss?" Cash persisted, ignoring Zeke.

"He's one of them in the lounge car. Or maybe the dining car."

"What's his name?"

"Sid Banning."

"Never heard of him."

"You will," said Zeke. "He's real smart."

"Prisons and Boot Hill are full of smart people like him."

"You can't—"

Cash loosened the red handkerchief from around his neck and gagged Zeke. "You talk too much."

While Miles covered the two outlaws, Cash removed the tiebacks holding the curtains away from the windows and trussed Zeke to the nearest strap hanging from the ceiling. Then he gagged Abe and tied him up as well.

"Okay, boys," Cash said, "you get to live, whereas most of your compadres probably won't. I suggest you stand real calm and don't misbehave."

He turned to the passengers. "Don't try any heroics. When the train stops, make for the rear, fast. Don't be alarmed, there are a couple of bodies back there. Get to the caboose and then get off before it moves again."

"Yes, Marshal," said a bespectacled man.

"Good." Cash turned to Miles. "All set for what's on the other side?"

"Always," Miles replied.

Cautiously, holding his Colt in readiness, Cash opened the door, again belabored by noise and wind-rush, and then stepped onto the short metal landing.

He found cold iron pressed against his nose.

The outlaw he presumed was Hoop grinned. "Drop your gun."

"Wouldn't you like that," Cash said.

A knife flew past Cash's ear and pierced Hoop's throat. He made a choking gurgling noise. Cash simultaneously knocked the pistol to one side as it was fired. The sound of the single shot was drowned by the noise of the wheels crossing the rail joints.

Hoop made more gurgling noises as blood drooled over his square-cut beard. He reached ineffectually for his throat.

Miles withdrew the blade and wiped it on Hoop's green flannel shirt. Hoop's eyes rolled back into his head. Without a qualm, Cash toppled him off the metal landing.

"I figured stealth was paramount and chose blade over lead."

"Good choice," Cash said, "but he may have killed me with that shot he got off."

"It was a risk I knew you were willing to take."

"Nice. Come on."

They entered the passenger car. This was the same as the last with a central aisle. There were eight men and two women, all gagged and tied up, lying awkwardly on the seats. As there was only the one outlaw in the car to guard them, Hoop or Banning must have decided it was easier to incapacitate the lot.

There was no time to free them, and not wanting them to get in the way, Cash showed his badge to the captives, saying, "We'll be back."

* * *

Cash and Miles stood in the small wind-blasted space outside the boxcar, one on each side of the interconnecting door.

Even over the din of the moving train, Cash could hear crashing sounds. He raised an eyebrow at Miles. His friend shrugged.

Then there were mumbled voices of at least two men.

Warily, Cash peered through the window in the door.

"What is it?" Miles mouthed.

Cash held up three fingers. *Three men.* He gestured: *fighting.*

Miles looked at his partner, drew his Colt and nodded, ready.

Cash opened the door and darted to the left, while he knew Miles would enter and head to the right.

His eyes widened and his mouth gaped. "Son of a bitch."

Miles frowned. "What the hell?"

A tall, dark-haired man bleeding from gashes on his face stood in the middle of the boxcar. His brown suit and paisley vest were rumpled from fighting, his black string tie askew. In one hand, he held a small dagger, blood dripping off its tip onto the wooden floor. His other hand gripped a smoking derringer.

Behind him lay two corpses.

The man turned and shot a glance at Cash and Miles. He remained in a fighting stance. His eyes roamed the two marshals up and down. Then the tension eased from his shoulders, and he grinned.

"I didn't realize I had an audience. Marshals no less."

When Cash and Miles made no reply, the man tapped his own chest. "The shape of your badges. U.S. Marshals. Very glad to see you both." A frown creased his brow. "I don't recognize y'all from the passengers who boarded the train." He pursed his lips. "How'd y'all get on the train?"

"And just who the hell are you?" Cash demanded.

The man's face brightened, and he took a step back into the doorway and swept his arm up in a flamboyant gesture.

"Calvin Carter, railroad detective." He bowed then gave them another broad grin. "Gentlemen, welcome to the *Sundown Express*."

CHAPTER 11

Medium Rare

"I could eat a horse, but I'll settle for a steer," Banning said, chuckling and rubbing his belly. "Come on, Miss Langtry, let's you and me eat." He held out a hand to her, the same hand that had slapped her.

She didn't dare gauge his mood. She knew she must act nonchalantly and show no fear. Bullies thrived on fear.

"What about the rest of us?" queried Gebhard, rising from his seat.

"I don't give a dead rat if you eat or not. But seeing as I'm feeling generous at the moment, I'll send in some food for you." A shepherding hand at the base of her spine, Banning escorted Lillie toward the door that led to the dining car. "Me and Miss Langtry want to eat in private."

"This is outrageous," growled Sykes. "This is *my* train!"

Banning glanced over his shoulder and shook his head. "Not anymore." He opened the door and followed her out. "Have a care as you cross over."

Not quite the gent, he didn't go first.

Though it was awkward crossing in her tight dress, she managed it without mishap. The gusting draught from the train's movement blew the lace of her bodice and sent her hair into disarray. She grabbed hold of the door handle and yanked it open.

Banning followed, shutting the door after him, and the relative silence from the raucous noise was welcome.

The tables all had place settings. The dining car was empty save for the outlaw called Prout, who stood as Banning entered.

"I'll see if I can rustle up the chef," Banning told her, striding over to Prout. "Release the chef."

"Yes, Boss." Prout hurried toward the galley door.

Lillie glimpsed the steel counters, pots and pans as he opened the door. She and Banning walked over to the galley doorway. Three men were tied up, sitting on the floor. Prout began unfastening the linen bindings.

"I want you to cook us two good steaks," Banning said. "One well done for me, one medium rare for the lady. With trimmings. All right?"

"Aye, sir," responded the chef, massaging his wrists.

"But first, fetch a bottle of wine for us."

"White or red, sir?" the chef asked.

"Do I care?"

"Should be red," the chef persisted.

"All right, if that's the case, bub, why ask? Make it red. Just get it, will ya?"

He turned to Lillie. "Damned staff these days, huh?"

She nodded noncommittally and sat at a table set for four. She eyed the silver knives but thought against concealing one. She might reconsider it if Banning drank too much to where his reactions slowed.

* * *

In the boxcar, with introductions out of the way, the three men sat on crates of whiskey while Carter apprised them of the situation as he knew it. While talking, Carter removed a whiskey bottle from an adjacent crate, opened it, and offered it to the marshals. Both declined. Carter shrugged. "I prefer brandy, but in a pinch, Kentucky rye will do. After the beating I just took, I need a little pick-me-up." He swallowed some of the whiskey.

He pointed at Cash and Miles. "How'd y'all get on the train? Best as I can figure, it had to be when we were in the tunnel. Given its speed, there's no horse that could catch the *Express*. Even if there were, you'd be shot long before you reach the caboose. So, how about it?"

Cash said, "Tell you later—right now, we've got more passengers to rescue."

"Are there more marshals?"

"Just us. And you."

"That's not a lot to go on, but what's the plan?" Carter asked.

"From what the Abe guy told us," Cash said, "there are two men running the *Express* and six more in the salon car."

"Plus the one on the train's roof. Miller," Carter said. "I heard his footsteps and saw him come inside the main car for a brief visit earlier."

"Is he wearing a blue shirt under a brown vest?" Cash asked.

Carter nodded. "Yeah, that's him."

"He, uh, lost his head," Cash said. "He got off the train in a hurry. We're still at six."

"We're coming up on the next station," Miles said, "but I don't think we can retake the train by then."

Carter nodded. "Banning is expecting me to deliver a message. Or, rather, the corpse I was supposed to be." He removed the envelope from his pocket and showed it to Cash and Miles. He tapped the paper. "If a body doesn't fly off this train, the boys up front will know something's not right."

Miles pointed to the Yates brothers. "We've got two to choose from here."

"Yeah, that's right." Pulling a fountain pen from his inside jacket pocket, Carter began writing on the envelope. When he finished, he got up and moved to the smaller Yates brother, Toby, who had a neat little bullet hole in the center of his forehead, complete with powder burns, courtesy of his derringer. He knelt briefly and tucked the note in the dead man's denim jacket. "No use straining ourselves with the fat one. Anyhow, this one's more my size."

Cash slid open the boxcar's side door and looked out.

The station was coming up fast.

"Time for the messenger service." He took Toby's legs and Miles clasped the man under the arms and hefted his torso. Swinging the body between them, they built up considerable momentum. "One, two, three!"

As the station began to whiz by, they let go.

They scarcely had time to see the startled look on the faces of the few people on the platform before the train had passed.

"Message delivered." Cash shut the door. "But we've still got a problem."

"Yeah." Miles nodded. "The outlaws'll be expecting the two brothers to be back."

"That's true," Carter said. "They'd head for the salon car, I reckon. But if we're thinking of surprising them," he gestured between himself and Cash, "neither of us has the build of Teddy."

Arms akimbo, Miles looked down at the remaining corpse. "Judging by the brothers' complexions, I just volunteered to go up top."

"Good point." Cash turned to Carter. The marshal tugged at the bandolier. "I put this on thinking we'd need extra firepower. Turned out one of the bandits thought I was their compatriot. Gave us a few extra seconds to get a jump on them. I can pretend to be Toby and maybe we can plump you up with flour sacks or something so we can pass you off as Teddy."

"Worth a try," Carter allowed.

"You armed, apart from that pop-gun?"

"I've got both of their six-guns." He held open his coat to reveal the holster strapped to his waist. One gun was holstered, the other tucked in the gun belt. "I'm a lefty, so I'll have to improvise."

Cash squinted at the railroad detective. "How long have you been doing this? We're talking real guns and bullets, not stage props. I don't want to have to worry about my back."

Straightening his tie, Carter grinned. "Don't worry. I don't get stage fright. Besides," he said, his grin dropping from his face, "I've got some payback to deliver."

Miles warned, "Just don't be so blind to that and miss something vital. "I'd hate to have to break in a new partner." He raised his eyebrows at Cash.

"That'll be the day," Cash said.

* * *

Banning had drunk half the bottle of red wine, while Lillie was still sipping her first glass. It was palatable, but only just. While they'd been waiting, Prout had been in and out with dishes of sandwiches for those in the salon car.

Finally, Banning said, "Ah, here he is. Don't take long, a good steak, eh?"

The chef came out carrying two large plates. Prout followed with two dishes: potatoes dusted with parsley and sage, and refried beans.

"Medium rare, ma'am," the chef said, placing it in front of her.

Prout lowered the vegetables to the table.

"Prout, you can high-tail it to the loco cab now. Take a sandwich for Krebbs."

"Yeah, good idea, Boss."

Lillie's filet was nicely browned, sprinkled with black pepper and partly covered with a pungent paprika-flavored cream sauce. She cut into it with ease, and it was pink inside. She continued to cut little pieces but didn't have the appetite to eat a bite.

Banning's rump steak was charred with a mustard-smelling sauce on the side. He forked a square into his mouth, then said sarcastically while chewing, "Glad to see you're enjoying it."

"I've had better," she commented.

"Funny lass, you are," he said, topping up her glass with wine. "You know, this might be your last meal."

She stopped pushing the meat around on her plate, displaying no outward concern to his continual threats. "What's your story, outlaw? Did your mum and dad not give you enough attention? Or was it way too much?"

"What in tarnation are you jabbering about?"

"Most men that are damaged freight can usually trace it straight back in a beeline to childhood. Neutered boys, you might say."

"You best watch your tongue, miss."

She crossed her arms and titled her head to the side. "Poor little mum's boy, is it?"

Banning eyes squinted, lit aflame by some internal fire. "Lady, you may walk with royalty, but you can't hold a candle to Ma." He leaned in over the table. "She was a nurse during the war and had the call to help a family sick with cholera when I was eleven. She was a good woman. Last I saw her, she was waving to me from the train window as I stood on the platform with my pa."

"I see. Sounds to me that your 'ma' just up and left you and your 'pa' outright. It's no wonder you have train issues."

"And it sounds to me that you should be minding your own business. Enough of all this nonsense about feelings and such." He sat back in his chair, seemingly unnerved by the fact that Lillie was able to evoke such a response, and turned the tables. "What about you? What burrs are under the saddle of the great Lille Langtry?"

"My sole lament will be not appearing as Lady Macbeth later this year."

"You're one plucky lady, I'll give you that."

"Give me your sidearm and I'll show you just how plucky I can be."

He slapped the table and burst out laughing.

CHAPTER 12

No Tomorrow

Cash turned the handle of the interlocking door to the passenger car, and it swung open onto a right-hand corridor with four private compartments on the left-hand side. Carter slid open the first that was occupied by three bound and gagged men.

Cash flashed his badge. "We'll be back for you shortly." The men nodded and seemed to visibly relax.

When Carter opened the door of the second compartment Cash was surprised to see four men and two women. Though ashen faced, they were all untied. He had no time to question that aspect. "I'm a U.S. Marshal," he explained.

"Thank God," said the redheaded woman, attempting to hold together her slashed clothing. He noticed splashes of blood.

"Are you hurt, Ma'am?"

"I will be fine, thank you." There were tears in her eyes and her chin quivered. "I am so very glad to see you!"

"Well, stay here for now. We've got a train to take back."

"Good," she said. "I hope that means you won't hesitate to kill them all."

He was taken aback by the vehemence in her tone. "We'll do what's needed to keep you all safe, Ma'am. For now, stay put." He shut the door.

Two more compartments contained more tethered passengers, all seemingly unhurt.

Cash and Carter crossed the gap between the two passenger cars and found themselves in another corridor on the right side of more private compartments. One at a time, Carter slid open the doors. More hogtied passengers.

When Carter opened the door to the last compartment, he exclaimed, "Miss Madison!"

She was conscious, and a big, bearded man was busy cutting away her cream chemise. The floor was littered with shreds of her white blouse and green velvet bolero jacket.

"You bastard!" Carter seethed.

Karl was already turning, the sound of the opening door having alerted him, knife glinting. His mouth gaped in shocked surprise, the stogie dropping to the floor. "Carter?" His teal-colored eyes seemed dead as he grabbed Jessica and raised the blade to her throat. Her face paled.

In the same instant Cash's bullet entered Karl's right eye and, when it bloodily exited his cranium, it shattered the big window behind.

Jessica stared in disbelief as Karl slumped to the floor. "Oh, my God," she breathed as Carter cut her loose and held her. "He...he..." Tears ran over her cheeks.

Cash said, "You must be the senator's daughter."

"Yes. Has...has the ransom been paid then? Is this nightmare over?"

"No, Ma'am. I reckon you should move to the back of the train, next to the caboose. You'll find a number of passengers there—and two outlaws tied up. We'll be back as soon as we free the other passengers."

She made her way to the door and stopped. "Take care, Mr. Carter, and thank you, both."

He gently patted her shoulder, compassion crossing his face. "I'm sorry none of us came to your aid sooner. Don't worry now, Miss Madison. We're taking back the train."

A weak smile flitted across her features.

Carter escorted her along the corridor to the end of the car. He opened the interconnecting door and helped her from one coupling platform to the other on the next car. "Just keep on going, don't stop for anyone," he said. "You'll be okay when you're with the others."

* * *

Returning to Cash's side, Carter said, "The next car is the salon. Last time I came through, there was a guy guarding the door. Name of Mule. Smells like one, too. He has a glass eye—left one—so that's a blind spot."

"How many more?"

"Hell, let me think." He counted them off on his fingers. "Only Greene and White, I reckon, but I could be mistaken. There may have been others I've never seen."

Cash nodded. "We'll go by your accounting: that makes four. We can ignore the pair in the locomotive cab for now."

"Those odds aren't too bad for a sharpshooter like you, Marshal. That was a hell of a shot you took, killing Karl."

Cash shrugged. He opened the car door and slid out, ducking, onto the metal coupling platform. Carter followed and shut the door after him. Cash crossed to the other car's platform and for a few seconds he peered through the window in the interconnecting door. He leaned close to Carter's ear and shouted, "No sign of a sentry here. I saw two guys standing at the bar at the far end."

"I reckon we're ready for the last act." Carter cocked his gun. "Open the door, Marshal."

Cash turned the handle, keeping his eyes on the pair at the bar. They were drinking and talking loudly, their backs to the captives, the handles of six-guns jutting from their holsters.

Carter followed him in and shut the door quietly.

Expecting the Yates brothers to be returning from the boxcar, neither outlaw turned because of the noise from outside in the brief moment when the door was open. But Gebhard did. He immediately recognized Carter and stood, a quizzical look on his face.

Carter raised a finger to his lips.

Cash flashed his badge and Gebhard nodded. Sykes was dozing in the seat next to Gebhard. Gently, he shook the train's owner awake and signaled for him to keep silent. Slowly, others captives noticed the newcomers and then anxiously eyed the two outlaws at the bar. The barkeep had swiftly taken it all in and backed away, moving slightly to the right of his two customers.

Reaching Gebhard's side, Carter whispered, "Where's Miss Lillie?"

"In the dining car," the manager replied, wringing his hands. "With Banning."

"Damn," Carter hissed.

At that moment the train entered the tunnel. The windows went dark briefly until the internal lights flickered on.

Mule Dunn eased off the bar. "It's getting tedious going back and forward all the time." He turned and leaned with his back and elbows resting on the bar. He spotted Carter and blinked, adjusting his eyes to the dimmer light of the lamps. He squinted and said, "Toby, what you doin' with the actor here? Last I hear, Banning tol' you to toss him off of the train."

Carter knew most people were not that observant. They never took much account of the clothing that friends and companions wore. Mule expected to see one of the Yates brothers, and Cash's build resembled the thin one they'd dumped off the train earlier. As already agreed on their way here, Carter affected the Arkansas drawl of the Yates boys and threw his voice in Cash's direction as if the marshal was speaking. "He's jus' tole us there's a money box in one of them compartments, b'longs to the actress. Where's she at?"

Out of the corner of his eye, Carter saw Gebhard's eyebrows rise. Even Cash cocked his head. He was close enough to detect the ventriloquism and seemed surprised at the excellence of Carter's delivery.

Mule moved from the bar and pushed his way through the captives. They parted like the Red Sea as he approached Carter, Cash, and Gebhard. He stopped a few feet from them frowning, his eyes squinting. Being short-sighted and having only one good eye was not a useful attribute for an outlaw.

Carter was half turned, Gebhard by his side, with Cash standing behind them, his head low in his collar. With his body as a shield, Carter detected the movement as Cash drew his weapon.

Time was up.

He turned back to Mule, full on, letting the other man get a clear look at his face.

"Eh? Carter?"

"What's wrong, cowboy?" Carter said in his own voice. "Don't you know a dead man when you see him?"

Mule's eyes widened. His hand cleared his gun from its holster.

"Down!" Carter shouted and snatched Gebhard's arm and hauled him to the floor.

That gave Cash the clearance.

Cash's single bullet blasted a hole through Mule Reynold's heart, spinning him to the floor.

In that same instant all of the captives either hid behind their seats or lay prone on the carpeted floor, while Emerson hunkered in a corner, scribbling notes in his notebook as if there was no tomorrow. Which was still a possibility for some.

The other outlaw at the bar leapt over the counter, using his gun butt to knock out the barkeep. Letting off a wild shot, he dropped behind the bar.

The train emerged from the tunnel into daylight.

"Don't be a fool, White," Carter called. "Give up."

Seconds later, bullets burst into the car from the skylight. The glass shattered and rained down on the passengers and the bar area. An abrupt rush of wind swirled into the car, lifting napkins, papers, and playing cards.

White stood up sharply, clutching his neck as blood poured out.

As White fell to the floor, a figure appeared at the interconnecting door to the right of the bar, smashed the glass window and began firing at Cash: one, two, three shots, all going wild.

"That's Greene," Carter called.

Cash fired and two of his slugs hit the hinge of the door and it swung open, doubtless confounding Greene.

Then before he could shoot again, Cash glimpsed a blur of motion outside.

CHAPTER 13

Meat Cleaver

Banning noticed Lillie's eyes widen. Dewy violet, mesmerizing. But she wasn't staring at him. She was looking over his shoulder, alarmed. Her lips parted but no words came out of that charming mouth.

Banning glimpsed movement in the reflection of the highly polished spare cutlery laying to the side on the table.

Instinctively, he ducked, rolled off his chair and landed on the carpet as a meat cleaver thudded down, missing him by inches and becoming imbedded in the pristine cloth and wooden tabletop.

Banning drew his revolver and fired, the shot slamming into the chef's shoulder.

The knife dropped as the man sank to his knees, gritting his teeth. His eyes looked beseechingly at Banning.

Banning leveled his gun.

"Please don't kill him." Lillie was on her feet beside the table.

His thumb carefully lowered the hammer. He slid the gun in his holster. Instead, he kicked the chef full force in the chin.

The man collapsed, unconscious, likely with a broken neck. "The only reason I didn't shoot this bastard is 'cause of you. Your reaction there probably saved my life," he said.

"While I'm grateful for your act of civility of my behalf, I regret that I let my stupidity and fear give away the chef's heroic attempt."

Banning's ire raised along with hand to strike her in the face as he had done earlier, but the popping of gun fire caught both of them by surprise at the same time.

"What the hell?" Banning shouted, quickly lowering his hand. He stepped toward the rear door, then stopped and turned.

Lillie stood immobile, hands on hips, watching him.

"Stay here," he snapped, though he knew she had nowhere to go. She couldn't very well jump off the train at this speed.

She ignored him and dropped to her knees to care for the wounded chef.

* * *

Miles swung down from the roof, his boots catching Greene full in the chest. The sudden blow sent the outlaw flying over the guardrail and off the train.

Cash and Carter rushed to the side window just in time to see the body flop in the air, hit some scrub, and then slide down a gully, dust scattering into the sky.

Still hanging from his perch, Miles let go and landed with a clang onto the metal plate of the coupling platform. He stepped into the car, grinning broadly, his arms outstretched. "How's that for a flourish, actor?"

Carter made a slight bow and eyed the broken skylight. "It looks like you brought the house down," he said, smiling.

Amid the sound of the windblast through the skylight and open door, the captives realized that the danger was past. They sheepishly regained their feet and looked questioningly at the two marshals, curiosity on their faces.

Carter introduced the owner of the *Sundown Express*, Warren Sykes, who stood and shook their hands.

Sykes straightened his rumpled vest and studied the badges on their lapels. "My Lord, I'm glad to see you!" Then, frowning, he added, "How did you get on board?"

"It would seem to be a secret," Carter said. He winked at the lawmen.

Cash didn't answer. Instead, he fired three rounds toward the door that still hung ajar. The shots smashed the glass of the other car's door and impacted somewhere inside the dining car.

Yet again there were shouts of alarm and curses from the captives. Most of them hunkered down and put their hands over their ears.

"What is it?" Miles asked, turning in a crouch and raising his gun.

"Saw someone coming toward us," Cash said, "peering through the door window."

Stooped and running, Carter joined the marshals. "Thick-set guy, black hair, handlebar moustache, wearing pin stripes?"

"Yeah, that was him," Cash answered.

"That's Banning," Carter said. "He can't be pleased."

Cash smirked as he reloaded. "You could say that. He lit out like a jackrabbit."

* * *

Breathless, Banning opened and shut the door into the dining car. He was surprised to see Lillie Langtry sitting at their hastily vacated table. She was smoking a cheroot. The chef still lay on the floor, but now his head rested on a rolled-up tablecloth and his wound had been bound with torn material.

"By the look on your face," Lillie said with absolute composure, "things are not going well for you. Isn't that a pity?"

"I reckon I've been double crossed," he seethed, reloading one of his pistols. "There were two strangers shooting up my men. I didn't see it all, but I'm certain they got Greene. Probably White as well."

"Guess the cavalry has arrived." Lillie inhaled a lungful of smoke, the cheroot's tip flaring brightly.

Banning paused a moment, frowning. His eyes glanced around the room and rested again on Lillie.

She breathed out smoke, crossed her legs, and straightened her dress.

"Can't figure where they came from," Banning said. "I'll have to leave you here. I'm going forward to the loco. Prout and Krebbs will be there. We can still control the train. The ransom money should be at the fueling station soon." He went over to her. "I so wanted you."

"Dead or alive?"

"Oh, definitely alive, Miss Langtry." He swiftly grabbed by the shoulders and pulled her in to kiss her.

Lillie's swing was unforgiving as she smashed the end of her cigar into Banning's right cheek.

The outlaw yelled and stepped back, his face intense with rage. Wiping the ashes from his face, he warned, "Miss Langtry, I will return and make you regret your action."

Lillie's violet eyes flashed anger back at him. "Others have tried," she said.

CHAPTER 14

Henry V

Cash glanced around. "There's been a lot of shooting. Is anyone harmed?"

The politicians shook their heads, but one of the journalists, Holtman, spoke up, "Bullet just grazed my arm. No issue." He gave the politicians a sour look. "I've had worse covering elections."

Emerson, the other newsman, knelt by the barkeep. "He's out cold, otherwise unscathed."

Gebhard tugged at Cash's sleeve. "What about Miss Langtry? She's with that fiend. What are you going to do?"

Cash didn't need reminding. He'd already wondered about seeing Banning by himself. What had the outlaw done with the actress? "We'll cross over to the dining car in a minute, sir."

"That's strange," Sykes said, pulling out a gold fob watch from his elegant boot. "It's about now the train reverses. I don't know why, but it does." He gestured at a window. "I've noted it most of the day, going back and forth. The same countryside features. And the tunnel."

"What's the time?" Cash asked.

Sykes consulted his watch again. "Six o'clock."

"Only about an hour to go until sundown," said Miles.

"They're headed straight to the fueling station," Cash said. "Expecting the money to be delivered."

"That's not so bad, surely?" said Sykes. "From what you've told us, you've freed the captives at the rear."

"Banning has a good idea that we've stymied his plans, and he has probably guessed that if we're here, the money isn't coming. In his demand he stated he has a number of accomplices waiting for him at the fueling station with more captives. When the train stops, we'll be outnumbered and they can take control again giving a final ultimatum for a ransom."

"Or," added Miles, "simply storm the cars and, if they have a mind, kill everyone."

"There won't be any ransom money, will there?" Sykes asked.

"No, sir."

Sykes smashed a fist into his palm. "We'll get hold of the weapons from the dead outlaws." He gestured with distaste at the corpse of White. "We can damn well put up a fight."

"Or," Cash suggested, "we can make sure the train doesn't stop at the fueling station."

As if in response, the train lurched under their feet.

Sykes rushed to the window and peered out. "It looks like we need to act now. We're slowing down. I can see the watering tank just up the line."

Carter moved to the damaged door. "Then we'd better make sure this train doesn't stop. Us three against the three up front: I like those odds much better."

"As do I," Miles agreed, then added, "Sykes, you and the others gather up whatever arms you can find and hold the rear here while we storm the front."

Sykes nodded as the trio hurriedly crossed to the dining car door.

Cash opened it and, gun drawn, stepped inside. Carter and Miles followed.

"Miss Langtry!" Carter exclaimed. The actress stood beside a table of half-eaten food. "You're alright?" He looked down at the chef lying on the floor. "Is he...?"

"We're both fine, thank you, Mr. Carter." She studied him. "To paraphrase Miss Hardcastle from the same play: 'I'm glad of your safe arrival, sir. It appears you had some accidents by the way.'"

He grinned. "I failed the audition for a corpse."

"I'm glad." She looked at Cash and Miles. "And these gentlemen have helped you, I take it?"

Carter said, "May I present the heroes of today, Marshals Laramie and Miles."

Cash touched his borrowed Stetson in greeting and added, anxious to get on, "Where's Banning, Ma'am?"

She waved toward the galley door. "He's going to the engine, Marshal. He has two more men there by the names of Prout and Krebbs."

"Useful to know for their tombstones," Cash answered and strode to the galley door.

"Can I do anything?" she asked in earnest.

"No, Ma'am," Miles said, keeping pace with Cash. "We're just pleased you've survived your ordeal. I recommend you head to the back of the train. You'll find Miss Madison there with other captives. They've gathered weapons and are safeguarding the rear cars from further assault."

"Very well," she nodded and smiled warmly. "I will do as you recommend, Marshal."

As they came upon the two tied up galley staff, Miles freed one with his knife, while Carter yanked at the binds of the second. They quickly helped the men to their feet.

"At the back of the train you'll find the other passengers. You'll be out of harm's way, and you can help if need be," Cash instructed them.

Next came the interconnecting door which opened onto the coupling footplate and, then more rolling stock, the tender which was stacked with coal. Beyond, the engine, its chimney stack belching.

A figure appeared atop the coal, two guns raised, then opened fire.

As bullets noisily ricocheted off the wall of the car, Carter yelled, "It's Banning!" He dove to the side, firing wildly in return, while Banning ducked behind a mound of coal.

Cash and Miles dodged back inside the doorway of the galley and out of the line of fire.

"He's only got twelve shots total," Cash shouted. "He's got to reload sometime. When he does, we rush him."

Two more shots from Banning. Both were wasted.

"I make that twelve," Miles said.

"Me, too," said Cash, quite used to counting an opponent's bullets while under fire.

The shooting stopped.

Carter, gun in hand, stood.

Banning abruptly emerged from the pile of coal and fired twice again.

Carter groaned and sank back down, grasping his left arm which had sprouted blood. He looked back to the marshals in reproach. "Unless, of course, he has a third gun."

Banning appeared. "Tricked you, Dandy," he said, angrily.

Cash looked to Miles. "Through the door."

Miles nodded, and said to Carter, "Stay down."

The pair of them darted through the doorway, guns ablaze. Chips of coal flew everywhere and then, above the sound of the engine, there was a loud yelp and continuous cussing.

They stopped shooting.

Miles reloaded, keeping an eye on the coal tender while Cash knelt by Carter. "You hurt bad?"

"Nope," Carter said, "but I'm sure it'll hurt like a bitch tomorrow."

Suddenly, a fusillade of shots sounded, coming from the engine cab, splintering the wood wall of the car behind Miles.

"Gideon!" Cash yelled to his partner who'd dropped into a crouch on the metal footplate.

"I'm all right," Miles said. "Two men, in the cab of the engine, one with a Winchester." He pulled a splinter of wood from his cheek and flicked it away like a toothpick. "I caught sight of the fueling station. We'll be there in a matter of minutes."

Carter spun open the cylinder of his gun and reloaded. "Gentlemen," he said, "how about a little Henry the Fifth."

Cash frowned. "What do you mean?"

Carter snapped the cylinder shut. "We few, we happy few, we band of brothers, it's time for a frontal assault." He pointed ahead.

Cash removed his borrowed hat and darted into the galley, coming out moments later with a long soup ladle.

"Planning on stirring things up, eh?" Carter said.

"Something like that." Cash put the hat on top of the ladle. "Here," he said, giving Carter the ladle and hat. "This should draw any fire."

Carter gave a slight chuckle. "I would be only too happy to distract your adversaries."

"Good. Miles and I will take care of the rest."

Carter hooked a finger through the leather thong of the hat, making sure it would stay suspended in position. "I'll give y'all until the count of ten." He crouched in readiness.

Miles and Cash kept out of the line of sight. "I'll take the left, you the right," Miles said.

"Yeah, I'm always right."

Miles grimaced and rolled his eyes.

Under his breath, Cash finished counting: "Eight, nine, ten."

As the first shot sounded, fired from the right-hand window of the loco's cab, Cash hauled himself up the back of the tender, clasping onto the metal side.

A second shot.

Cash raised his head carefully, air and dust whipping at his face.

A third shot.

He screwed his eyes to mere slits and looked over the banked collection of coal. He saw the gunman, leveling his rifle on the windowsill of the cab. Either Prout or Krebbs, he didn't know or care which.

A fourth shot.

Holed twice, the Stetson flew into the air and was gone.

He glanced to his left. Miles was scrambling over the coal. Then he stopped moving and rested his gun arm on the coal, steadied his aim. He must be sighting on the other outlaw leaning out from the left-hand window.

Cash steadied himself and aimed. It was still a good distance away, but possible.

Miles fired, and seconds later Cash squeezed his Colt's trigger.

The outlaw on his side fell forward and tumbled onto the tender coupling platform. Maybe he was only winged. It didn't matter, because a moment later he let out a scream and fell under the wheels.

"Got mine, too," Miles said. He started shimmying over the rest of the coal, gun pointed ahead, closer to Cash now.

That should leave only Banning in the cab.

The train's whistle sounded and the brakes were applied and the tempo of the pistons reduced. The train was slowing.

Miles raised his head a little and swore. "Sweet Jesus."

"What is it?"

"Have a look."

Cash saw no less than five men with rifles and handguns lining the rooftops of the small train station and a few even hung from the ladders of the water tower. They appeared alert. They must have heard the gunfire. To one side of the station, a couple of men on horseback appeared to be guarding the access to the small town of Sydney's main—and only—street. A bullet-riddled stagecoach stood nearby, the team of four horses still in their traces idly grazing. There was no clue as to the whereabouts of the stage's passengers. They were supposed to be held captive, maybe in the station building.

Just a few hundred yards ahead, three men were trotting toward the engine, ready to grab the handrails and board. Extra guns. More threat.

CHAPTER 15

Shards

Banning forced the engineer to ease the throttle of the *Sundown Express*. He looked out the small window. It was a huge relief to see his three compadres making their way to the train. At last, reinforcements. He waved, recognizing them. "Shorty, Elmer, Mack, we got troubles!" He wasn't sure what was happening in the back of the train, but he was sure that, given enough men, any problem could be eliminated.

He also recognized the two horsemen, Monty and Bragg. As instructed, they barred access of the townsfolk to the fueling station.

Knowing that his three men would be able to leap onto the train before it made a complete halt, Banning told the engineer to brake at the water tower.

With a gun in one hand, he pivoted and stepped out onto the coupling platform, scanning the tender for those unwelcome guests who had taken out Prout and Krebbs.

He jolted on hearing a familiar, sing-song voice: "Banning!"

Scowling in annoyance, Banning looked up at the tender and saw the actor man standing there, a six-gun in one hand and a soup ladle in the other. That oddity gave him a moment's pause.

Behind Carter the sky was painted red and yellow, the onset of sundown.

Deadline.

He shielded his eyes and squinted up at Carter. "I don't know how you bested the Yates boys, Dandy, but it's now curtain time for you!"

"Oh, really?"

"If I don't get you now, my men from the station will."

"They're not going to make it that far," Carter said, his tone disconcertingly full of assurance.

"You reckon? And why not?"

"Your third mistake." Carter pointed to the sky. "You forgot to look up."

Frowning, wary that Carter might be attempting a distraction so he could gun him down, Banning glanced at the station rooftop, but was none the wiser. Then, he heard a deep droning sound, like a huge swarm of bees. Some inexplicable shimmering movement in the sky caught his attention.

As if by a conjurer's wand, what appeared to be a flying boat materialized out of nowhere.

It was like an apparition, only parts of it visible. A craft of some sort with two wings jutting from the main hull.

Alarmingly, he saw a lengthy gap lining the craft's side. And poking out from the gap were rifles held by uniformed troopers who were firing.

The outlaws at the fueling station were taken completely unaware. Several fell off the top of the station's roof. Two men on the water tower returned fire and Banning heard what sounded like shattered glass.

His heart sank when he saw Shorty, Elmer, and Mack reach the loco engine only to be picked off by the overhead Army sharpshooters.

With his mouth hanging open, fury boiling up from within, Banning turned back to face Carter. Now, two other men, one white, the other black, stood next to the actor. He'd seen them before, briefly, just a glimpse in the dining car, before one shot at him. Their badges glinted dully. He backed away and grabbed the fireman's arm, using his body as a shield.

"What the hell is that thing?" Banning yelled.

"It's a secret," said the white marshal, grinning.

* * *

"I can't stay here while there's all this shooting," Senator Madison shouted. "My daughter's in danger. I'm climbing down now."

"Senator, stay here," the professor called. "It's dangerous!"

"Dangerous? I've been in my share of gun-battles in my youth, Professor." He opened the hatch and dropped the rope ladder through. "It's more dangerous flying in this damned contraption, if you ask me."

Unsteadily placing his feet through the hatch hole, the senator's toes located the rungs and, his frock coat flapping, he started gingerly climbing down.

* * *

The *Sundown Express* shunted to a halt just beyond the station, almost alongside the water tower.

As steam hissed and the pistons went silent, both fireman and engineer hastily jumped to the ground, abandoning the engine, and ran toward the rear of the train, away from the shooting.

It was pandemonium with bullets flying everywhere, caroming off steel, smashing into flesh.

Banning hunkered down in the cab as slugs pinged off the metal.

Miles jumped to the ground, somersaulted, and then drew his gun and started firing at the outlaws on the station platform. He made for a large cluster of dense green needle grass.

Carter clambered back over the coal and descended to the coupling platform linking the tender to the galley. From here, he was relatively protected as he engaged the outlaws manning the station.

Halfway down the ladder, Madison was hit. His face contorted in pain, he thrust an arm through a gap and clung on. He seemed incapable of going up or down. He just hung there.

Cash leapt from the top of the pile of coal to the roof of the engine cab. Then he jumped onto the top of the engine casing, avoiding the valves, and ran further along, careful not to slip. Tantalizingly, the end of the rope ladder swung just above the engine. He hopped onto the central of three domes, which gave him added height and reach. "Hold on, Senator!" he called above the raucous noise of guns.

The two outlaw horsemen next to the station—Monty and Bragg—had by now turned their mounts and drawn their rifles from their saddle scabbards and were targeting the troopers, high above. More glass broke and shards rained down to earth.

From the salon car, gunfire erupted, aimed at the outlaws at the station.

The horsemen continued firing until Bragg's steed was hit and collapsed, trapping him under its immovable bulk. Monty steered his sorrel toward the train, looking for Banning.

At last, Cash caught hold of the bottom rung of the rope ladder. "Hang on, I'm coming up!"

Without warning, there was an immense explosion of bright yellow.

The blast threw Cash backward and he lost his grip, went flying off the engine's roof. He landed in a dense patch of sagebrush, scratched and bruised but otherwise unhurt.

Slightly dazed, he lay there for a few seconds and stared in disbelief.

Soldiers shouted in shock while flames burst out and upward, licking at wood and balloon material. Several troopers jumped from a great height to their deaths.

Cash got to his feet. He could feel the heat from the flames. The rope ladder dangled freely. He couldn't see the senator on the roof or on his side of the engine.

The air vessel lurched and all of its structure was now visible, a jumbled construction of wooden slats, countless mirrors that smashed noisily with the intense heat, the metal of a steam engine and pipes clanging as the whole thing crashed to earth on the other side of the train.

Smoke billowed, climbed into the darkening sky.

In the glare of the flames, Cash saw Banning jump off the coupling platform. He landed, stumbled, his derby hat flying, and then ran down the slope toward the last rider. "Monty, give me a hand up," he shouted. "Let's get the hell out of here!"

Cash went for his Colt but it wasn't in his holster. He spotted it at the base of the sagebrush.

Monty wheeled his horse around and reached down, clasped Banning's outstretched hand. "What the hell was that thing?"

"God knows." Banning swung up behind Monty.

"What about the money?"

"There ain't any. Now, ride!"

By the time Cash recovered his gun, they were out of range.

CHAPTER 16

Corpses

Miles sprinted to Cash. "You alright?"

"I'll live," he said, shoving his Colt in its holster and dusting himself down. He glanced at the stagecoach. "I'm going after Banning."

Miles made to join him.

"No, Gid, you're needed here. Look to the survivors. See if you can find the senator." He pointed. "That fire's spreading."

Miles turned to look at the rear of the *Express* where people were clambering out of the passenger cars. He nodded and said, "I think you're right. You be careful, ya'hear."

Cash raced to the stagecoach, and after checking that the trailing traces were fastened, he checked inside. "Those bastards." Sprawled on the seats were the bloody corpses of two men and a woman. No driver or shotgun rider, their bodies were probably lying on the trail.

He had no time to haul the bodies out. He climbed up onto the driver's box and released the brake lever. Snapping the reins, he guided the horses to turn the coach, following the dust kicked up by the escaping outlaws.

The coach wasn't the swiftest way to travel, but he had the power of four horses—and two men on one horse were going to be eventually slower.

* * *

The flames from the downed airship were encroaching upon the train's engine. Miles rushed to the water tower base and climbed up the sturdy wooden ladder.

Once on the upper platform he had an uninterrupted view of the area of devastation on the other side of the train. The scene was like a fantastic depiction of Hell. Pockets of fire blazed, lending an eerie flickering incandescence. Strewn everywhere, bodies shorn of clothes, some charred, and among them a few still living but severely burned or without a limb or two.

He hurried round to the hose outlet and hooked it toward him. Normally used to replenish the loco's boiler, now he directed the spout at the flames and triggered it.

Water spray gushed out and some fires were immediately extinguished, accompanied by the sound of hissing steam.

While directing the spray, he surveyed the area and stopped when he saw green suspenders showing through the torn back of a black frock coat. Senator Madison was lying prone a short distance from the engine.

Miles directed the water at the flames until there was no water left in the tank.

Then he clambered down and ran round the front of the engine, and reached the senator.

* * *

The shooting had stopped. There was no more opposition it seemed as Carter looked out from his place on the coupling platform. A few outlaws were still alive, groaning, clutching their wounds, but posed no real threat. Three were running toward the town, hats flying off their heads in their haste. The rest of them were scattered across the station roof and the surrounding ground as grisly corpses.

He coughed on the smoke and tucked away his gun. The wound on his left arm had dried. The pain was merely a dull ache. He turned to check on the passenger cars.

It appeared the majority of passengers had disembarked and were milling together, their voices rising as he approached. He heard several talking about the explosion, and some pointed to the smoke and the remnants of fire, while others began patching up and giving comfort to the wounded.

His eye caught sight of Lillie, and he noticed she was pushing Jessica ahead of her, which he found odd.

When he reached them, he saw that Jessica had a cut lip and appeared sullen. Lillie held one of Jessica's arms up her back.

"What is this all about?" Carter asked.

"She hit me!" Jessica exclaimed, trying but failing to shake off Lillie's grip.

"With good reason, my dear, as you very well know," Lillie said. "On my way to the back of the train, I purloined a bottle of liquor from the goods wagon, or boxcar as you Americans call it. I thought I'd cheer up me and Miss Madison." She sighed. "Well, by the time I got to the passenger car, Madam here had released one of those bandits. I was sure she was going to let loose the other one as well."

"I was not!" Jessica turned to Carter. "You believe me, don't you?"

Before he could reply, Lillie went on, "I didn't have much time to think things through, but I knew I couldn't take on both of them. So, I had to sacrifice the bottle of bourbon atop the man's head. After that, I convinced Jessica it would not be in her best interest to continue with her actions."

"I see where this might be going," Carter said.

"I'm sure you do. I used the broken bottle to slash her skirt." She indicated the place, along Jessica's right side, where a large rip showed Jessica's cream petticoat and a thin line of blood on her thigh. Lillie raised her chin. "You and your two marshals can have those two brigands and this one." She pushed Jessica at Carter. Once divested of the senator's daughter, Lillie adjusted her dress.

She then gasped in alarm. "Mr. Carter, your arm—you're wounded."

"It doesn't hurt much. I was lucky." Gently holding one of Jessica's arms with his right hand, he said, "Was the man she freed called Abe?"

"Yes," Jessica mumbled.

"I thought so." Carter said. "He tried to stop Karl from taking her away."

"He isn't all bad, really," said Jessica, softening her tone.

Carter shook her head. "He is one of the outlaws. It isn't for me to determine guilt or innocence. He needs to face the full force of the law for what he and his accomplices have done. Where is he now?"

Lillie pointed. "There he is."

Abe had his hands tied behind his back and was being pushed ahead of a handful of men. A streak of dried blood trailed down one side of Abe's face and had dripped onto his buckskin shirt leaving behind stained splotches.

CHAPTER 17

He's a Dead Man

Dusk fell, with a full moon rising from low purple clouds. Droves of crickets chirruped in the distance sparse vegetation, going silent as Cash passed. The trail Banning and Monty left behind was clear enough, since the dust had hardly settled. He knew the coach was gaining on them. He could vaguely see the outline of a horse carrying two riders making for a broad cluster of rock. With visibility dwindling steadily, washing away color and definition, while the moonglow created deceptive shadows, Cash needed to move posthaste.

The horse stopped, and one of the riders dismounted. He wore a hat so it must be the one called Monty. Banning sat on the horse, leaning his hands on the saddle horn.

Monty walked a few paces forward, then stopped. The stance he adopted suggested he was going to shoot.

Cash urged the team forward, faster, producing a moving target.

The wheels bounced over stony ground, the horses' hooves churning up prairie grass.

A shot rang out and the near lead horse in the team collapsed, falling against its companion in the traces.

Within seconds, the horses collided with each other, and the stagecoach lurched and tumbled sideways. A wheel struck something unforgiving and it shattered with a splintering crash. Horses squealed.

Still clasping onto the reins, Cash was lifted into the air and landed jarringly on the upturned chassis, knocking the wind out of him. His hip immediately felt sore, and he sensed bruising on his shoulder and left arm.

One of the bodies from inside had been tossed out of the stagecoach and landed with a thud next to him.

Two of the horse team had managed to regain their feet and stood placidly, still tethered by the reins, while a third lay on its side, entangled in the traces and neighing in distress. It possibly had a broken leg. The fourth was dead.

As Cash hauled himself upright, he heard a weapon being loaded. He glimpsed Monty walking slowly toward the wreck, rifle raised in readiness.

* * *

"What a mess," Monty said under his breath as he jacked another shell into the chamber of his Winchester. He glanced over his shoulder. A few yards back, Banning sat astride the horse, watching and waiting.

No money, no more gang to speak of. What in tarnation went wrong? This has to be Banning's fault, and after he took care of the marshal, he'd deal with Banning. He was owed big-time.

He stopped walking as he spotted the lawman standing up beside the wrecked stagecoach. *Some tough hombre*, he thought. Probably still dazed after the crash. No matter. The man is as good as dead.

Raising the rifle to his shoulder, Monty aimed and fired.

But the lawman didn't drop.

He was certain his shot had hit him. Monty continued forward, shooting again. This time he saw the man stagger back and yet he stayed upright.

What the hell? Monty fired again.

Finally, his target collapsed. But a gut-churning feeling swept through him. He'd been had.

Another man was standing still immediately behind where the first had fallen, moonlight glinting off a metal badge. An actual dead man had been taking the bullets for the marshal—the swine had used the corpse of a passenger as a shield.

"Jesus!"

Before he could aim, he felt the pounding of two bullets in his chest.

Monty exhaled. He tried raising the rifle, but all strength had left him. Breath had left him.

He sank to his knees and fell face first into the dirt.

CHAPTER 18

Grave Tidings

Carter stood by the *Express*, one hand gripping Jessica's arm, the pair of them illuminated by the lights from the passenger car. He saw Miles approaching alone. "Ah, Marshal Miles," he called. "You're..." He didn't finish, for even in the poor light he'd noticed the grim features of the approaching lawman. "Is Cash all right?"

"Yes, he's going after Banning." Miles half turned on his heel and gazed back at the front of the train, the thin trail of smoke blending with the encroaching night sky. "Most of the troopers we came with died in the explosion or the fire."

Carter nodded.

"Senator Mad—" Miles began, then eyed Jessica.

She looked at Miles. "Papa? What about Papa?"

"He came here with us," Miles said.

"Came...but..." Her brow creased.

"I'm sorry," Miles said, "your father's dead."

Jessica went limp and would have dropped to her knees if Carter hadn't been holding her. He let her down gently and she knelt on the ground.

"No, no," she wailed.

Despite her apparent attachment to the one outlaw, Carter was not without pity. She had just learned the most terrible news. The detective bent over her with an attempt to comfort her. "He died thinking not one iota less of you."

She seemed inconsolable as she shook in his grip and her voice trembled. "I want to see him."

* * *

Cash leaned down and grabbed the Winchester lever-action shotgun from the stagecoach's boot. It was loaded.

In the near distance, Banning sat watching, no doubt debating whether to stay and fight or run.

Cash went over to the horses.

First, he checked on the animal lying in pain. It was obvious by the way its foreleg appeared twisted, it was broken. A section of protruding bone confirmed his diagnosis. He gently stroked the horse's snout and forehead, then stepped back and put the poor beast out of its misery using the rifle.

The two horses standing flinched and became restless. He tucked the Winchester under his left arm, then withdrew the knife from his boot. He cut the harness and collar, freeing both horses. Grasping the mane of the chestnut, he swung up onto its back. Holding the reins with one hand and the shotgun with the other, he found the chestnut responded well to the pressure from his knees and heels. He led the animal toward the pile of rocks.

While he'd been attending to the horses, he'd kept an eye on Banning. He'd seen the outlaw skirt around the rocks, heading west not more than a few minutes ago. He had decided to run.

Cash's mount was sturdy, one of the coach's two wheelers, the pair being the largest and strongest of the team, used to provide stability. His animal seemed to like to ride free of its harness and rode like the very wind.

Before long, he began closing the distance with the outlaw.

CHAPTER 19

Carnage

Holding onto Jessica's arm, Carter followed Miles toward the front of the train. Lillie tagged along, concerned about the actor's wounded arm.

They crossed the rails a little beyond the cowcatcher.

A moment later, they reached the senator, who was lying face-down. A patch of blood showed on his back.

"Are you sure you want to see him?" Miles asked

Biting her lip, she nodded.

Miles knelt on one knee and turned the senator over. The right side of his face had suffered severe burns with most of the skin blistered, while the left was unblemished. His single eye was shut. Miles had seen to that on discovering the body.

Jessica gasped and sank to her knees. She stroked her father's singed hair. "Oh, Papa, I'm sorry, I didn't mean for this to happen."

Miles said. "I'm not sure how much you knew or what part you played in today's activity, but it's sure suspicious. Care to enlighten us?"

"No." Her features twisted in anguish.

Lillie stepped forward and placed a hand on Jessica's shoulder.

Jessica flinched. "Don't touch me!"

"You owe it to the memory of your father to tell the truth," Carter said with an air of kindness.

Jessica gulped, her resolve weakening. "All right, it doesn't matter now. Nothing matters now." She took a long moment and then began. "I fell in love with Abe Stone. When he told me he was in an outlaw gang, I saw a chance to do what Nelly Bly does. I would be a part of their gang, write stories about them, and get information for a series of sensational articles..." She paused and sobbed.

"Go on," Carter said gently.

"Abe played me. Like a fool, I believed he was interested in me. He was convincing. He said he and his pals wanted the *Express*'s route and timetable. I asked him why and he told me they'd just do a holdup, nothing too serious. Nobody would get hurt." She sighed. "I was a fool. I took the information from my father's correspondence. Abe gave it to Banning. He...he did the rest." Her glistening eyes were beseeching. "I didn't know they planned to kill anybody...I didn't know."

She raised a hand and wiped away the tears from her cheeks.

Miles thought either this girl was telling the truth or she had taken acting lessons from Lillie Langtry.

"But after you'd seen what they'd done," Carter said, "why did you attempt to free those two outlaws?"

"I only intended to release Abe. Even then, I thought I loved him. When we were cooped up back there, Abe pleaded, said he wouldn't do anything like this again. My father, if he had known about…Abe…" Clearly, she couldn't go on. She was racked by tears.

Her heart seemed to be breaking in front of them.

Carter helped Jessica to her feet and cast a querying look at Miles. "She has paid for her foolishness, don't you think?"

Miles replied, "It's not my call to make, but I do appreciate your candidness, Miss Madison. That may be in your favor. For now, let's go into town and see about making some arrangements for your father."

Jessica continued to sob while she took Miles's arm and went with him.

Lillie watched the pair walk away, and when they were a fair distance, she said, "Such a shame. I wouldn't want the poor girl to go to the bastille, but I don't feel she should get off scot-free either." She turned to Carter and looked at the blood on his arm. "I do think I should tend to your wound. May I call you Calvin?"

"Only if I may call you Lillie," Carter replied lightly. "I would be forever beholden to have the famous Miss Langtry as my nurse. As soon as I am bandaged up, we'd best join forces in seeing what we can do to help the others who've been injured as well."

CHAPTER 20

Coffins

Rocky promontories jutted into the night sky. Shale and chalk clattered under the chestnut's hooves. The strident songs of countless crickets persisted. Dark fingers of prickly pear cactus loomed, like sinister sentinels. The full moon illuminated the terrain, but it was a false friend, casting many deep shadows, any one of which could be a fissure capable of causing a sprained fetlock. Cash let the chestnut find its own way, while steering it on Banning's trail.

Ahead, two hundred feet or so, was a dense forest of lodge pole and limber pine trees. Once Banning entered that, he'd be more difficult to track.

He was close now. The outlaw was about a hundred feet in front, his horse tentative also. Cash reined up. He raised the shotgun to his shoulder. Black powder smoke wafted in his face as he loaded another shell.

The explosion echoed around the rocks, rebounded. His chestnut shifted its feet but otherwise remained steady. The nearby crickets stopped.

Banning slid off his mount and disappeared into the shadows.

Cash gently urged the chestnut forward.

The crickets started up again and sage-scented night breeze drifted by.

When he was roughly ten feet away, Cash halted the horse and dismounted carefully. The ground was a mixture of sand, shale, and slate. Treacherous. Not to mention his footsteps would be heard.

He held the shotgun in readiness and walked forward, eyes searching ahead for the slightest movement. Every few feet, he'd stop and listen. He didn't want Banning doubling back and stealing the chestnut, or attacking from behind.

Banning didn't have a rifle. Monty had used that. So, Cash presumed the outlaw was left with only two .45s. He had no way of knowing Banning's marksmanship, but he figured he was about to find out very soon.

* * *

With Jessica by his side, Miles had walked into the one-horse town of Sydney. He hadn't expected many places to be open, given the hour, but the gun battle and the explosion must have stirred up considerable curiosity as many residents were milling around and discussing the nature of the events.

Miles asked for the location of the telegraph office. With help, they soon found it, and the office's lights were still on. Miles stepped onto the boardwalk and opened the door. The bell jangled above.

A young man rose to his feet at the counter.

Miles nodded to the clerk. "I'm U.S. Marshal Gideon Miles and I have to make some high priority cables."

The clerk noticed Jessica in the doorway, eyes widening at the sight of her slashed clothes.

She entered reluctantly and sat on a bench by the window.

First, Miles sent a brief situation report to Chief Penn in Cheyenne. Then he sent a message to nearby Fort Sydney, requesting troopers and wagons for the dead. He turned to the clerk. "Does the town have an undertaker?"

"No, though the barber is willing to grave dig for a modest fee."

"What about carpenters?"

"Yes, we have several carpenters."

"One coffin will do. It's for this lady's father."

"I'm terribly sorry for your loss, miss," the clerk said to Jessica then turned back to Miles. "If you stay here, Marshal, I'll go get Baker. He's the finest at his skill and has made quite a few coffins in his time."

"That would be helpful. I reckon Mr. Baker and the others will find themselves very busy over the next few days."

* * *

Banning gritted his teeth. Jesus, the lead that peppered his left side and shoulder stung like hell.

That damned son-of-a-bitch had gotten closer than he'd realized.

He hunkered down behind a boulder, shivering, and peered ahead but couldn't see a thing.

The marshal was no fool, he wasn't going to show himself against the lighter night-sky. Wisely, he'll keep low, blend in with the darker surroundings.

He could hear footsteps on the rocky surface. His mouth went very dry and gritty, as if he'd eaten sand.

The footsteps stopped. Followed by silence. Not even crickets.

Minutes dragged and he heard nothing. He wiped sweat from his forehead and winced at the movement.

As pain gnawed at him, his stomach roiled. That steak threatened to erupt from his gut. Hell, he should have taken the actress as a captive. With her as cover, he wouldn't be in this predicament. Then again, maybe he was better off bullet riddled than listening to her chatter on about his ma and pa. Even if she had pinned him. His ma never came back. She took up a new life with the doctor tending cholera patients, leaving her only son with a broke heart, a drunk father, and years of beatings.

But it all happened too fast. He still couldn't believe what he'd seen in the sky.

Nearby, the crickets had taken up their chorus again.

"Banning! This is U.S. Marshal Laramie. I'm here to take you in. Come peaceably and you won't get hurt further."

Go to hell! Banning bit his tongue, almost tempted to shout in reply to taunt the lawman. But it would be foolish to give away his position as the marshal had just done. Banning grinned. *There.* Over to the right, about twenty feet, if that.

He aimed his right-hand Smith & Wesson and, slowly, quietly, cocked the hammer and fired three times.

CHAPTER 21

No Regrets

Cash saw the flashes from Banning's pistol, bright in the darkness, over to his left. He responded with two quick blasts of the shotgun.

Banning grunted, and Cash heard the outlaw fall with force.

Treading with care, Cash moved forward, aware he still had two shells left in the shotgun.

He saw Banning lying on the ground, breathing noisily. Beside him was a single .45. His other revolver was in his holster.

Cash kicked the .45 out of the way and stood over the outlaw, shotgun ready.

Lead pellets had made a mess of Banning's chest and upper torso, and had shredded an ear and part of his cheek.

"How come I missed?" Banning rasped. Then he saw Cash's bare feet.

"Something I learned from my Arapaho family." He had a pair of moccasins in his saddlebag that he used when stealth was necessary. Since that was left behind at Area 53 with his horse, he had to settle for bare feet. As soon as he'd spoken to Banning, he moved silently several paces over to the right. Banning fell for the misdirection and shot at the empty spot he'd been speaking from and, in the process, advertised his own position. Cash's ruse was not without cost. The jagged shale had cut into the soles of his feet, but he'd clenched his teeth and endured the pain.

Kneeling down, he removed Banning's second six-gun from its holster and flung it away.

Banning's breathing was irregular now, and shallow. "This...isn't how...how I planned...it."

"I suppose not. It was a daring plan," Cash conceded. "There's one aspect I want you to tell me about."

"Why...why should I tell...you anything?"

"Because I can make your dying easier or harder. It's up to you."

Banning sucked in air and winced as he did so. "All right, lawman...what do you want to know?"

* * *

Astride the chestnut, Cash rode up to Joni's Saloon, trailing behind him Banning's mount which carried the outlaw's body. Pale yellow light and loud voices spilled out of the doorway. Dismounting, he looped the reins over the hitching rail and, with boots back on yet limping as both feet were still sore, he stepped up to the batwing doors.

On the wall above the bar the glazed eyes of a stuffed elk head stared out at him. The only person who seemed interested in his entrance was the sturdy barkeep, his furtive eyes quick to judge whether a newcomer was liable to cause trouble. Cash flashed his marshal's badge and the barkeep switched his attention back to pouring drinks. Two saloon girls drifted between tables, serving. A number of men he recognized from the rear passenger car were drinking and talking.

A glum Warren Sykes was seated at a table drowning his sorrows with a tankard of beer, while the four politicians were at the next table talking in low voices, each with a glass of amber liquid in front of them. Cash didn't see Miles.

"Marshal Laramie," Sykes called, beckoning him over.

Cash hobbled to the man's side. "Sir?"

Gesturing at Cash's feet, Sykes said, "Are you alright?"

"I'll survive. Have you seen Marshal Miles?"

Sykes nodded. "I believe he's at the Hampden Hotel across the street. I'm on my way over there now. I can let him know you're looking for him."

"Thanks."

"Did you get Banning?"

Cash nodded. "I wouldn't be back otherwise, Mr. Sykes."

"That's a relief." Sykes finished his beer and stood to leave.

Cash made his way to the bar and ordered a whiskey. He drank it straight away, paid, then left.

The street was deserted. The townsfolk must have had enough excitement for one day and went home to recover from the trauma.

Passing the corpse of Banning slung over the saddle, Cash reflected that the outlaw had wasted his life, believing in the illusion of easy gain instead of the truthfulness of honest work. Sure, Cash performed his duty as required and felt little pity for outlaws like Banning. After all, his sort didn't spare a thought for their victims. He knew Miles felt the same. True, a small scrap of humanity was lost whenever they were forced to take a life. Each, in their own way, swallowed the unease at snuffing out a life, any life, and buried it deep, and holstered their weapons, and moved on. It was what they did.

He crossed the street, stepped up onto the boardwalk and opened the door of the hotel lobby. A man at the front desk said, "Good evening, sir. Do you require a room?"

"I do. Name's Cash Laramie."

"You're fortunate, Marshal." He pushed the register round for Cash to sign. "We've taken a big influx tonight, but I have one spare room."

Cash signed and noted several familiar names. "Is the other marshal in his room?"

"No, sir. He's with several people from the train." He pointed across the foyer to a set of double doors. "They're all resting in the lounge before dinner is served."

"Thanks. I'll mosey on in, then. That's one more for dinner, if you will."

"Right away, sir. I'll tell the head cook."

As he entered the lounge, he saw it was occupied by Sykes, the two newsmen, Miles, Jessica Madison, Calvin Carter, Lillie Langtry, and her manager, Mr. Gebhard, all sitting on upholstered chairs or sofas, some of them holding desultory conversation, others simply meditating, one or two with eyes shut.

"Marshal, you're back!" exclaimed Lillie.

He waved.

Miles looked up at him and raised a questioning eyebrow.

Cash nodded. "He's out front. Slung over his horse. Banning's had his last ride."

Miles blew out a long breath and rubbed his face. "Well,"

he said, "that's that."

Wearing a sling on his left arm, Carter stood and walked over. "Glad you made it, Marshal." He shook Cash's hand and then spun on his heels, spreading his good arm wide. "Now that we're all together, something's been troubling me. How did Banning and his men even gain admittance onto the *Sundown Express*?" He eyed each person in the lounge one by one. "The only answer seems to be they had help from someone on the inside." Carter let his words sink in before continuing.

"Now see here, Carter," Sykes blurted out, "what are you implying?"

Carter shrugged. "I'm implying nothing. I'm stating facts. You and the other bigwigs were a natural group to ride the inaugural journey. As the owner of the *Express*, you would obviously be a passenger. The same could be said of poor Mr. Halsworth. Miss Langtry brought her star status with her, ensuring newspaper coverage across the country."

He winked at her. She offered him a demure grin.

"Where Miss Langtry went, Mr. Gebhard always followed." He inclined his head to the manager. Gebhard, for his part, shifted in his seat and straightened his back.

"To help tell the story of the *Sundown Express*—and sell future tickets—Sykes made sure to have a pair of newsmen on board." Carter gestured to Emerson and Holtman.

Holtman frowned. "But Banning and his gang came from the passenger cars."

"Precisely."

"How were those invitations distributed?" Lillie asked. She, too, had sat up straighter, scooting to the edge of her seat.

"By lottery," Carter said. "Every person who rode in the passenger cars today did so because their names were pulled from the bowl and read aloud. It was a contest. Everyone had bought a newspaper, filled out their names on an entry blank, and returned it to the newspaper office. Then, in a very public ceremony, the editor of the *Cheyenne Leader* pulled a name out of the bowl. He handed it to his reporter who read the name aloud. The editor's daughter then wrote down the name on a bill that was then posted for all to see."

Gebhard screwed up his face. "I don't see what you're driving at, Carter."

"Don't you see," Lillie said, her face bright with understanding. "The only person who truly knew the names on the entry blank was the man who read out the names." She beamed up at Carter.

The actor held her gaze for a long moment, a quizzical quirk of a grin showing on his face. Without breaking eye contact with Lillie, Carter said, "Isn't that right, Mr. Emerson?"

"Don't be absurd." Emerson quaked. He bolted to his feet. "Are we going to take the word of an actor?"

"I was an actor." Carter reached behind his belt and pulled out his badge and pinned it on his lapel. "But now, I'm a railroad detective."

"This is preposterous," Emerson blurted out. "I hadn't seen those men before today."

"Not true. You may not have seen all those men, but you had met Banning. I noticed you recognize him when he first entered the salon car."

"You are mistaken," Emerson persisted.

Cash chimed in. "Actually, he's not." All eyes turned

toward the marshal. "That's what Banning told me before he died."

Carter opened his palms, shrugged, and offered a self-satisfied smirk at Emerson. To Cash, the former actor said, "Your presentation could use some work when the spotlight's on you. Add a little flourish and panache."

"The spotlight isn't for me. I'm just satisfied putting men like him behind bars." Cash gave Carter a bemused grin. "Besides, I can tell you enjoy it for the both of us."

Emerson stammered, trying to form words, then sighed resignedly as Miles took the handcuffs from his belt and secured the reporter.

Holtman chuckled, "Looks to me like I have another exclusive article."

Emerson groaned.

Carter inhaled deeply and let out a satisfied sigh. "I always enjoy the end of a case. Well, ladies and gentlemen, my arm is aching, so I'm going to turn in."

"You must have something to eat. I will bring a plate to your room," Lille said.

"That's very kind of you," Carter smiled at her offer and moved to the foot of the staircase, resting his sling arm on the newel post. With his free hand he gave Cash and Miles a little salute. "It was a pleasure working with you, gentlemen. Thanks for the help. Perhaps we can meet again sometime, in a less hazardous situation."

"As long as it isn't on a train," Cash said, "I'll look forward to it." He returned Carter's salute.

The actor turned and climbed the stairs.

Lillie laid a hand on Gebhard's arm. "Frederick, dear, it has been a trying day. I'm going take dinner to Mr. Carter and turn in myself."

"Do you want me to—"

She shook her head. "No, I don't believe so. Call for me in the morning, will you?"

Gebhard pursed his lips and then with ill grace nodded. "Very well."

Lillie stood and made her way to the staircase. The higher she climbed, the faster she moved.

Cash went over to Miles. "What happened while I was gone?"

"The cavalry is gathering wagons from the townsfolk and working with them to clean up. Mr. Sykes told us the train is inoperable and it needs to be cleared from the tracks. They want to get it done fast—other trains need to pass."

"We'll have to get our horses from Area 53."

Miles nodded. "Which reminds me," he said. "There's no trace of the professor."

"The explosion completely destroyed every vestige of him?"

Miles shrugged. "Who knows?"

"Perhaps it's for the best," Cash said. "Maybe he was ahead of his time. *The Pegasus* was a clandestine project and the thing isn't supposed to exist."

"It doesn't now. But it makes you wonder what other secrets they've got hidden away in those Area Fifties sites."

"Well, Gid, this secret has few witnesses left. Almost all the outlaws who saw it, sadly, are dead—as are the troopers who flew with us."

Cash Laramie halved his smile. "Flying like a bird was most thrilling, my friend. But I reckon I'll stick to horses from now on." He slapped his partner's arm and started walking to the door. "Come on, food can wait. The saloon's calling. I think we both deserve another round of drinks."

†

ABOUT THE AUTHORS

David Cranmer writes Westerns under the pen name Edward A. Grainger. He is the editor of BEAT to a PULP books and webzine. His work has also appeared in *The Five-Two: Crime Poetry Weekly*, *Live Nude Poems*, *Punk Noir Magazine*, *LitReactor*, and *Chicken Soup for the Soul*. David is a dedicated Whovian who enjoys jazz and backgammon. He can be found in scenic upstate New York where he lives with his wife and daughter.

Scott Dennis Parker lives, works, writes, and listens to music way too loud in his native Houston, Texas, with his wife and son. He is the Saturday columnist at DoSomeDamage.com and has a long-running blog at ScottDParker.blogspot.com. Learn about his other books at ScottDennisParker.com.

www.beattoapulp.com